The Asking Price

by the same author

Superintendent Kenworthy novels

THE SUNSET LAW
THE GREEN FRONTIER
SURRENDER VALUE
PLAYGROUND OF DEATH
THE ANATHEMA STONE
SOME RUN CROOKED
NO BIRDS SANG
HANGMAN'S TIDE
DEATH IN MIDWINTER
DEATH OF AN ALDERMAN

Inspector Brunt novels

MR FRED
DEAD-NETTLE
GAMEKEEPER'S GALLOWS
RESCUE FROM THE ROSE

JOHN BUXTON HILTON

The Asking Price

A Superintendent Kenworthy novel

St. Martin's Press
New York

For information, address St. Martin's Press, 175 Fifth Avenue, New York, N.Y. 10010.

Library of Congress Cataloging in Publication Data

Hilton, John Buxton.
The asking price.

I. Title.
PR6058.I5A9 1983 823'.914 83-9607
ISBN 0-312-05660-5

First published in Great Britain in 1983 by William Collins Sons & Co. Ltd.

First U.S. Edition

10 9 8 7 6 5 4 3 2 1

CHAPTER 1

Kenworthy hadn't wanted the job and had talked his way out of it. Forrester hadn't wanted it either, but had let himself be talked into it. He and Kenworthy were as unlike each other as any two in the Met. Forrester had come up through the Sweeney, had let the slogging and slugging rub on to his reputation without getting himself involved in the things that got talked about. He was a man who got his way in unlikely places and was known to hate wasting time. No one expected him to enjoy himself, or to last long, wearing out his trouser-seat in the Cabinet office.

It was a new section that had been created, a glorified information bureau: 'research' and contingencies. The same work had always gone on; this was just a new guise for it. Kenworthy and Forrester had brought up the same reason for begging out of it: politics. Bransby-Lowndes, liaison officer between ministers and the new team, said that that was unthinkable. No government could survive the suggestion that party machinations were being paid for by the Treasury.

Which brought up another point. The Opposition would oppose it when they got to know it was happening. So as soon as they got back—

'They'll retain it,' Bransby-Lowndes said. 'You'll have made yourselves indispensable. It isn't politics; it's government. An administration needs something like this, whichever way the electorate has jumped.'

Bransby-Lowndes, top of his year in the Administrative Grade admissions, was said to have been uncertain about turning his back on pure academics. He called his new toy the Faculty and ticked off the advantages over a desk which, like the rest of his office, was empty of anything.

Some claimed that that showed an orderly mind.

'No Judges' Rules. No QCs hectoring you in the witness-box. No A.10 sifting nugatory complaints. To all intents and purposes your own choice of personnel, not necessarily restricted to serving members of any department. No enquiries into your methods: if we didn't trust you, we wouldn't be making the offer. Allowances on the First Division scale. Operational expenses the highest in your profession. Paperwork down to the minimum. Access to high places—'

'Including the Prime Minister's private and personal carpet?'

'I doubt whether the Prime Minister would ever hear of you by name,' Bransby-Lowndes said thoughtfully, as if he were considering the point for the first time. 'You'd get your work from me, tell me your answers. You might, just now and then, be called in to speak to a member of the Cabinet. A personal chat sometimes saves time, ensures clarity.'

'*Now and then*,' Kenworthy said. '*To all intents and purposes—within reason*—all the usual small print.'

'You'd not be expecting to be offered a dictatorship, would you, now, Kenworthy?'

The tone of that jibe settled the issue there and then for Kenworthy. It was the tone of a mind that he thought was on the small side for a potential academic.

'Obviously you've already got a few files ready to throw at me if I do take it on. What are they?'

Bransby-Lowndes laughed like an up-and-coming minor general spotting the enemy's plan.

'Not on your Nelly!' Something about the archaic slang seemed to underscore the man's high-power insincerity.

'But I'll give you fictitious examples. Case one: the Home Secretary is under pressure to re-open a murder case twenty years old. A mental defective was hanged for it late in the 'fifties. He wants to know in advance what the result will be if he does review it. Case two: the Treasury has alternative schemes for de-indexing Civil Service pensions. One of the Sunday heavies has leaked them: find the source. Case three: a whizz-kid Private Parliamentary Secretary, lifted off on a scintillating career, has just had a trip to Acapulco that he couldn't afford. Who paid?'

'I thought crime was sordid,' Kenworthy said.

'Don't you go about talking at Rotary lunches about the magnetism of the truth?'

'That doesn't mean digging it out so it can be more effectively suppressed.'

Bransby-Lowndes looked at him with his eyelids screwed up against his own cigarette smoke.

'Think about it.'

Kenworthy did—and said No. He worked out his last handful of years at the Yard—not happy years. The Yard was not as Kenworthy had seen it when he had joined. Forrester was appointed to Whitehall—Kenworthy did not know by what flattery. He barely bothered to wonder how Forrester had made out. He and Forrester had never been close. Governments changed: the Faculty survived. Kenworthy retired, was alternately bored or mixing himself up in something or other. Then Forrester sent for him.

Forrester was different. He was wearing a suit of a cut in which he had certainly never been seen in Victoria Street. He was progressing from Squad muscle to swivel-chair fat. His office was utterly unlike Bransby-Lowndes's: wire baskets spilling out tatty manilla folders. He told the switchboard to put no calls through, but one was too urgent to be kept waiting. Kenworthy listened to Forrester's end of it: vexatious—and Forrester contemptuously familiar with the inner circle. But then, he always had a way of letting his peers see how he was doing.

'Impressive,' Kenworthy said.

'They keep me at it.'

'I'm glad I left it alone.'

'Oh, I don't know. There are kicks. It isn't corridors of power—it's passages of panic. How did an internal minute, the marginalia dynamite, get into a reporter's hands? Not for action—just for knowledge. A German weekend rag of lesser breed has printed a canard about someone not unknown to the throne. Question isn't *is it true*?—but *how did they know*? And ought a twenty-year-old indiscretion of a professor of divinity to debar him from a bishopric? In other words, is anyone ever likely to find out?'

'Charming,' Kenworthy said. 'When do we get your *Memoirs*?'

'I've got a ploy for you, Simon.'

'That depends.'

'Of course it depends. Let's look for some lunch.'

They ate Italian in Old Compton Street. The last time they had lunched together it had been, at Forrester's insistence, off public bar shepherd's pie, washed down by cask bitter in Camden Town.

'Let's have it,' Kenworthy said. He wanted no *parvenu* attempt by Forrester to float into it from elegant small-talk.

'Morley Mortain.'

Kenworthy laughed. 'That's got you all beat, hasn't it? If you ask me what I think—'

'Simon, we *are* asking you, very seriously, what you think.'

'I think it was pre-arranged—a package deal.'

'That, of course, has been considered. And I'm sorry—it's not on. There couldn't have been that amount of collusion.'

'I only know, of course, what I've read in the papers.'

'The papers have been four-fifths of the trouble.'

'What would you want me to do? Spy on former colleagues?'

'No. Just look at it. Look at it *all*. See if you have any ideas no one else has had. We need a few new ones.'

'Tempting, Jack. Hewitson's been handling it, hasn't he? Would he know that I was involved?'

'Yes and no.'

'Thanks for the clarity. It would have to be part-time only—and strictly my own time. And no suppression of files.'

'What do you think we are, for God's sake?'

'I know only too bloody well what you are. And I'd need help—my own nominations.'

'Nominate.'

'Shiner Wright.'

'I was afraid you'd ask that. Sorry, Simon. Shiner's serving a second apprenticeship with the Fraud Squad.'

'Shiner, Jack.'

'All right. I'll try again. Anyone else?'

'Wait till I see the colour of it.'

They did not walk back to Whitehall together. Kenworthy wanted to go to Foyle's. There was spring sunshine in the Charing Cross Road. He watched a young man in an *Up-and-Under* sweatshirt slip a paperback into his back pocket.

CHAPTER 2

Morley Mortain is a village on the Bedfordshire-Buckinghamshire borders. Its manor was given by William to one of his marshals in 1066, just before the Conqueror turned south on London. In the twentieth century there has been infilling with prosperous villas, attracted by the nearness of the motorway. And there has grown up a reasonable tolerance between a new type of resident and the earthier mortals who live in the red brick rows of the Duke's model nineteenth-century cottages. The village also offers asylum to a salting of retired bourgeoisie, and has the usual ration of former officers of field rank. Thirst is catered for by a tavern at either end. The Green Man, which is almost all public bar, and the Magpie, which is almost all recently annexed restaurant. At times of spiritual drought, Morley Mortain can flock to the Church of St Lawrence, Early English, vicar the Reverend Miles Yealland, young and even younger-looking. Or they can sing hymns of bold metaphor to simple march rhythms under the corrugated vaults of the Gospel Hall, pastor the very poor and even poorer-looking Albert Saxby.

It is as well that the social strata of Morley Mortain have a natural leaning towards tolerance. Their tastes, aspirations and political faiths are broadly based. The floor of the Green Man, no longer sawdust-strewn, but bare of any covering but a darts-mat, is staunchly Conservative. It is only to one or two houses with five-figure incomes that the *New Statesman* is delivered. The Reverend Yealland has been alleged to pray silently for his inner thoughts to be forgiven when Pastor Saxby is singing one of his celebrated solos in the adapted Nissen hut that has given Chapel Lane its name. These renderings, a great draw to some of the cottagers, are apt to cause Commander Broad to falter at the lectern within robust stone walls fifty yards away.

But Morley Mortain lives effectively in harmony, and that is a good thing, because it was a generously varied cross-section of the population who were spirited away from the village one invigorating March morning.

The Reverend Miles Yealland was one of them; so was Albert Saxby, neither of them praying or singing at the moment of abduction. So was Mrs Commander Broad, as the cottagers called her: the Commander was believed to have met her in Portsmouth, before the beginning of his rise from the lower deck. Mrs Brenda Ogilvy was with the party, the young married woman from 'Les Hirondelles', who was so wrapped up in herself and her two-year-old Jason that she seemed to be walking on a cloud from which she was aware of nothing and no one. From Morley's lower declivities there was Herbert Spriggs, the well-known bingo-caller; there was Rita Lonsdale, whose love of mankind had enabled three of them to father children on her. And from somewhere in the village's uncharted middle, there were Millicent Mayhew, who kept the craft shop, and Dolly Mason. It was not immediately that Kenworthy was able to differentiate sharply between them all.

On this Monday morning, a black van from one of the lesser-known security companies pulled up outside Dolly Mason's shop. No one believed that Dolly Mason was standing by to receive a consignment of bullion. It was assumed that the personnel of the van, on their way to some bank, had stopped for tobacco. It was keen observation on Morley Mortain's part to have spotted that the van belonged to an unfamiliar agency. Later enquiries established that it did not belong to any known company at all. It was an *ad hoc* van, the only van of its kind, prepared by mechanics and signwriters for this single venture. The county police mounted a massive and man-consuming enquiry. Later, a nationwide investigation, commanded by Hughie Hewitson, whom Kenworthy had respected as sergeant and inspector, took a sweeping look at garages, lock-ups, parking spaces and signwriters' workshops. Result: nil. Which suggested that the money behind the exercise had been lavish.

The security guards had been wearing, in addition to their steel helmets, protuberant chinguards, and had had aggressive coshes hanging from their belts. An original touch had been women's nylon stockings pulled tight over their faces. These, in conjunction with helmet-rims worn almost at nose level, made working descriptions deficient. Moreover, no sooner were the men in the shop than they tilted sub-machine-guns forward from under their armpits. They then invited all the shoppers to accompany them in their vehicle. That is to say the Reverend Michael Yealland, who had come down to enquire about the non-delivery of his *Church Times*; Pastor Saxby, who needed cough-lozenges after his previous evening's performance; Mrs Commander Broad, who was nearly seventy, but made up like a thirty-seven-year-old trying to appear twenty-five; Herbert Spriggs, who had called in for cigarettes on his way to the surgery to renew his bronchial bottle; Rita Lonsdale, who was looking over a newly arrived batch of Mills and Boon's; Millicent Mayhew, who wanted change for the milkman; Brenda Ogilvy, whose Jason was filling his pockets with sweets from the counter; and Dolly Mason.

The black van was exceeding the speed limit before it had gone far along the Morley Mortain street, but then it stopped so abruptly that it rocked on its axles and the Reverend Miles Yealland descended at gun-point closely followed by Jason Ogilvy.

What had happened, the vicar described to the constabulary, was that one of the guards, catching sight in the driving mirror of his thin line of High Anglican clerical collar, had pronounced the words, 'Christ, not a bloody devil-dodger!' and had declared him unsuitable for the expedition. Pastor Saxby was wearing no outward sign of his status, and did not draw attention to it. The vicar came back along the street holding Jason by one hand, the child having been evicted because of his raucous screams. The nearest mobile police force was at Ampthill, some ten miles away, and by the time mobility was achieved, the black van had disappeared from the sight of observant man.

And so had its passengers. Ten days later, Commander

Broad received, in a plain packet posted in West Central London, an ear-ring which belonged to his wife, and had been worn by a great-aunt before her. Chief Superintendent Hewitson told the press about this delivery. He was relieved to have anything to tell them at all. There seemed to be a sinister implication in the intimacy of this jewellery—which the papers fully exploited. But when the first public shock had subsided, there was still no explanation of the kidnapping.

The strangest feature of the abduction was that none of the usual organizations would acknowledge having had anything to do with it. They got in touch with various editorial offices, using the code-words with which they habitually authenticated their messages. The IRA strenuously denied involvement, as did their undercover opponents over the border. The Red Brigade, the Palestinians, Iranian factions, were indignant that they should be suspected. Special Branch confidently assured the Home Secretary that neither the Libyans nor the Baader-Meinhoff rump were active in rural Bedfordshire. It is true that both Commander Broad and Justin Ogilvy received illiterate demands for ransoms, but these were eliminated by Hewitson's team as coming from unintelligent opportunists, who could not furnish details of the most elementary relevance; and who in any case could not possibly have had the funds to mount such a logistically intricate operation.

The media talked to the vicar, who seemed oddly disappointed to have been excluded from the excursion. They talked to Commander Broad, who seemed to think that this sort of thing would not happen if every able-bodied man in the country were in the Royal Navy. They turned their cameras on to Justin Ogilvy as he warmed up a convenience meal for Jason in their Habitat kitchen. His mother-in-law, who had come over from Watford to do for them, was kept occupied in another room while this was going on. The Outside Broadcasts unit went the round of the cottages, where they interviewed Rita Lonsdale's mother, a jolly and unharassed woman, who talked to the reporters with her three grandchildren on her lap, all sucking dummies. She seemed to harbour no resentment of her daughter's moral elasticity and facile fertility.

Mrs Herbert Spriggs believed that the whole business had something to do with the Unions, who were getting at her husband because he had always refused to join them. That was all she could think. Millicent Mayhew and Albert Saxby had no one to speak for them, and viewers had to be satisfied with a shot of the dusty curios in the window of the boutique, and of a knot of would-be worshippers gazing idly at the padlocked door of the Gospel Hall. Micky Mason bemoaned the fact that he was having to maintain Morley Mortain's only shop and paper-round single-handed. But as they said in the Green Man, 'As long as he's too bloody mean to bloody well pay for bloody outside help, he'll bloody have to, won't he?'

Then, one month and three days after their disappearance, the wanderers returned. They came with the April dawn, on foot as single spies, severally along the various approaches to the village. All except Albert Saxby. He did not return, even later in the day; and those who had shared this fugue with him made noncommittal comments and endeavoured to change the subject when his name was mentioned.

The public found it difficult to understand why no price had apparently been paid for the deliverance of the party. There were some tasteless scenes when the TV cameras panned in on tearful reunions. But no one explored in depth the histories of misery, of uncertainty, of suspense, the nearness that the hostages must have come to despair. Even their next of kin probably tired of their conversation in the day or two after their return.

CHAPTER 3

Now the superstar by-liners arrived with cheques that were worth holding up to the camera. Stuart Morris of the *Globe* was said to have gone to five figures for Rita Lonsdale, despite her reputation for letting anyone have what he wanted for nothing. She may or may not have been able to recognize her biography as Morris saw it: the wide-eyed Goldilocks whose lashes moistened at the reminder of her parting from Maureen, Doreen and Noreen.

At the time, Kenworthy had desultorily scanned such of the reports as came his way. Now he got hold of back files and tabulated common features and variations. In many ways it was difficult to believe that the six people had undergone the same experience in the same place. Their prison seemed to have ranged from a Turkish seraglio to a luxury bed-sit. REST CURE FOR NAP VICTIMS, headlined Ed Pownall, in the *Sunday Herald*. *Busy Herbert Spriggs*—he did not mention that Spriggs had been on what he called 'The Club' for six weeks preceding the outrage—*found time during his terrifying experience to catch up with his reading.*

'I've never read so many books in my life,' he told me in the snug little sitting-room of his modest Bedfordshire cottage. Mr Spriggs added that he had read a book once before, during the war in the Desert, but that an appointment with Rommel (Spriggs had been an RASC storeman in Cairo) *had prevented him from ever finishing it.*

On one thing the victims were agreed. They had been well treated. *We were well treated*—Spriggs. *We were well treated*—Dolly Mason. *I wouldn't mind being kidnapped again*—Mrs Broad. *They gave me everything a woman could desire*—Rita Lonsdale. *I asked for all Barry*

Manilow's records, and they were beside my bed when I woke in the morning.

It is surprising how one's field of taste can be enlarged. I discovered Hindemith and Bartok—Millicent Mayhew.

It was just like being in hospital—Herbert Spriggs. *They came round with tomorrow's diet-sheet, and you could have anything you wanted. I had steak and chips twice a day for a week.*

Nothing was too much trouble for them—Dolly Mason. *Rita Lonsdale had trouble with a broken plate, and they brought in a dentist.*

Albert Saxby was the other subject on which there was consensus.

MISERY-MAN FAILS TO RAISE ANTHEM FROM ORDEAL VICTIMS, Ed Pownall's sub-editor had sub-headed. *He tried to get us to sing 'Hold the fort, for I am coming'*, Rita Lonsdale had reported.

He really did not enter into the spirit of the thing at all—Mrs Broad. *I mean, there are times when you have to make the most of your predicament, aren't there?*

GOSPEL MAN LEANS ON PROPHET, was Barrington Watts's banner in the *Examiner*. Kenworthy knew Watts from past press conferences in the field, a gin-and-tonic man at the fag-end of middle age and of most other things. Reading between the lines, he had been overwhelmed by Millicent Mayhew's volubility. Even journalistic invention had been inhibited.

The prophet Amos lived on wild sycamore seeds and hated the sinful luxuries of the great cities. Mr Saxby was forever quoting Amos at us.

Kenworthy decided on balance that Millicent Mayhew would probably be his most fruitful point of entry into the fray. He was also tempted by Brenda Ogilvy, whose husband had savagely shut the door even on offers of cheques. The hardest sell had often the biggest profit-margin; but Kenworthy told himself to opt for the quiet life.

'Yes? Oh, dear—not another man from the papers. I promised Mr Watts—'

Kenworthy told her who he was, letting her think by innuendo that he was who he used to be. She was between two ages, and not too far beyond the first of them, but a woman who had given up—if she had ever bothered—any attempt to do anything about herself. Her hair was pepper-and-salt cut in a straight fringe. She was wearing a grey cardigan with the maker's label sticking out at the back of her neck. Her buttocks and thighs filled her dark blue slacks to capacity. But she had eyes of an almost angelic blue that had quick understanding in them. She led Kenworthy through her front-room shop: Filipino basketwork, Chinese wood-shaving figurines, clodhoppingly heavy coffee-ware by a potter in a neighbouring village.

'Ridiculous, isn't it? I don't take a pound, some weeks, and now since all this, I can't get enough supplies. I even sold a crocheted dressing-table runner of the Princess of Wales. A ghastly thing, not a bit like her. Honestly, I feel like slipping out of the back every time I hear the doorbell.'

They went into her living-room—amateur watercolours of willow-fringed meadows. Wild flowers—yarrow, campion and oxlips—in a table-vase. A biscuit-barrel, open on a folding tin tray-table on the hearthrug. Mozart was issuing from the irrationally spaced speakers of a music-centre.

'Only Elvira Madigan, I'm afraid. They've no Hindemith in Bedford or Bletchley. Now, what can I tell you?'

'Everything.'

'Oh dear, not all of it again? I couldn't believe my ears when Mr Watts told me what his paper was offering. I tried to stipulate that I was to have the final say in what was actually to be printed. He said there wasn't an editor in Fleet Street who would concede that, but he did promise a proof and what he called off-prints. I expect he forgot.'

'I expect so,' Kenworthy said.

'Well, they drove us out of the village after they'd rounded us up in Dolly Mason's, and then as you know we stopped to put off the vicar and that horrid spoiled child. Then the man in the passenger seat pulled a screen down, and for half an hour we were travelling in pitch darkness, bumping and jolting about. That was the nastiest part.'

'For half an hour or so? Were you able to judge from twists and turns which way you were being taken?'

'At first. But after a few minutes I was lost. I'm sure the driver was doing U-turns just to fool us. I thought that once we went into a lay-by and reversed after we'd come out of the other end. Then we obviously left the metalled road and came to rest. And they made us get out, and we were in a sort of brick-lined tunnel. They made us get into another van—a dirty, light green old thing, with no trade markings or anything. I did remember the registration numbers, which I told to Mr Hewitson—but I don't think they can have been genuine. Can I make you a coffee?'

'I'd love one.'

She went on talking as she moved about.

'Then another long, sick-making ride—between two and three hours. For a long stretch, I would say from our speed, and from the sound of other vehicles, we were on a motorway, most of the time in the fast lane. We arrived at a country house—well, a sort of country house. I'd say from its style it was built in the 'sixties. Not unlike a Mediterranean villa—the sort of place you see on the hills above Menton. I tried desperately to guess from the landscape where we might be. I thought it could be Wiltshire, from the white stones in the soil. But that might only have been the sun on them. And they fairly bundled us indoors. Obviously they didn't want us to see.'

Kenworthy did not know what brand of instant powder she had used. He did not remember ever having drunk worse coffee.

'You'd think this place had been built for the purpose. The bedrooms were on three sides of a square, looking down into a high-walled rose-garden, and our dayrooms were on the floor below. The aspect was very pleasant, and we had access to the garden, but none of us caught a view of the outside world.

'The rooms were beautifully furnished and our hosts, whoever they were, were most apologetic for the discomfort of our ride. They said they would do everything possible to make up for it. And I must say, everyone was kindness itself. I told Mr Watts, it must have cost a fortune, the way they looked after us. Books we asked for were produced in a day or two. Music. Choice of food and wines—'

'Television?'

'Yes—in two of the dayrooms.'

'Which channels were you on? Which region of *Nationwide*?'

'Oh, you are clever, Mr Kenworthy. Mr Hewitson asked us the same question. We weren't allowed to have *Nationwide*—or any other regional programme. You see, they were clever too.'

'And must have been pretty heavily staffed. Tell me about the staff.'

'Mostly men, one or two women. Youngish. Nearly all foreigners. They could have been Italians, Spaniards, Southern French—again, a Mediterranean impression.'

'And those you refer to as your hosts?'

'Disembodied voices. We never saw them. They made announcements to us over speakers. Charming people—most reasonable and understanding.'

'Could you initiate conversations with them?'

'We had a house-phone in each of our bedrooms and could contact reception: a most helpful young lady.'

'So by and large you got used to a number of voices? I expect Chief Superintendent Hewitson tried you out with a few samples?'

'He made each of us spend hours listening to tapes.'

'And no joy?'

'Mr Kenworthy, Mr Hewitson has the most *agonizing* way of not letting you know what he thinks.'

'You think you'd recognize the voices again?'

'Without fail. But do you know, I should hate to, Mr Kenworthy. All the time I was listening to the tapes, my fingers were crossed. I've read somewhere about the psychology of kidnapping – the rapport that grows up between captors and captured. I'd hate to be the one to make trouble for those people. They were so *nice*, Mr Kenworthy. It's difficult to believe that they were up to no good.'

'That's what you were meant to think.'

'But no harm has been done, has it?'

'Yet.'

'How can harm be done now that we've all been released?'

Kenworthy kept his counsel for a moment, and the blue eyes accused him.

'You policemen love to be mystifying.'

'Don't you find the episode mystifying, Miss Mayhew?'

'I've given up trying to puzzle it out. Looking back at it now, there was a sort of magic about it – something that doesn't come twice in a lifetime. When the Voice suggested that I should try the *Requiem*, it opened up a seam of new experience for me.'

'You made what I think it's correct to call a Freudian error just now, Miss Mayhew. You said you'd all been released. What about Pastor Saxby? Why didn't he come back with you?'

'That isn't for me to say, Mr Kenworthy.'

'You do want to be helpful?'

'I wish to remain jealous of my neighbour's reputation.'

'I would have thought that the pastor's reputation was as unassailable as any in your party.'

She tightened her lips and kept them tight.

'Or was it? Were there some curious goings-on, Miss Mayhew?'

'If there were, they happened in private.'

'Did you take this line with Chief Superintendent Hewitson?'

'I simply refused to surmise.'

'What was Saxby up to?'

'He was difficult at first. He tried to make us all sing. *"Throw out a lifeline, someone is sinking"*—And he was terribly critical when one by one we decided to make the most of a bad job and accept what compensation was offered.'

'He didn't go for the fleshpots himself?'

'Not at first.'

'But he limbered up later?'

Millicent Mayhew smiled thinly.

'You mustn't put words into my mouth, Mr Kenworthy. Let's say Albert Saxby does have his human side.'

'Have you read Somerset Maugham's *Rain*?' Kenworthy asked.

'You mean about the missionary who had fun and games? I don't think you ought to draw conclusions, Mr Kenworthy.'

'Footsteps in the corridors at night? Informatively stealthy?'

'Who was to tell whose footsteps they were?' Miss Mayhew said.

'More than one party, you mean? Isn't that another way in which they trapped you all? Would it be true to say that they provided such grounds for blackmail that none of you is now prepared to tell us the whole truth?'

She resolutely said nothing to that.

Kenworthy sat back and looked at her with the penetrating interest of a man who was never satisfied that he knew all there was to know about people.

'A month, Miss Mayhew: that was a long time. Yet the only impression I get is of a small group coming back as if they had been away on a planned holiday. It can't have been like that—not quite.'

'No, not quite,' she said, with one of her watery philosophical smiles. 'But don't you find that human memory is mercifully selective? Otherwise wouldn't we all be in mental homes? A woman separated from her only child; another cut off from her business, being mismanaged by a husband she knows isn't very clever. Even Herbert Spriggs wondering whether he'd lost his bingo connection for good. Of course we were nearly demented, some of the time. But did you ever talk to an old soldier? One who seemed to remember nothing of five years of war—except what he and his friends had found to laugh at?'

'I'm an old soldier myself,' Kenworthy said, and moved sharply back to business.

'When did Saxby cease to be with you?'

'He was simply not with us when they brought us away.'

'You mean he vanished overnight?'

'He had dinner with us—but not breakfast.'

'Did you know overnight that you'd be leaving in the morning?'

'They didn't announce it. They just suddenly took us.'

Kenworthy toyed with his next question—then asked it.

'Miss Mayhew—are there some people in this village today who wouldn't be too happy if they suddenly saw Albert Saxby reappear?'

She took time over her answer.

'I don't think that thought will help you very much, Mr Kenworthy. If he said nothing, the others wouldn't either, would they?'

CHAPTER 4

Kenworthy reported back to Forrester.

'Oh yes, there was obviously a relaxation of morals,' Forrester said. 'Herbert Spriggs is known to some as the Morley Mortain Bull. Rita Lonsdale needs to keep herself in practice. Hewitson says he doesn't think Justin Ogilvy will ever find his wife quite the same again. Mrs Broad never has ceased to hanker for the dockyard gates. And I wouldn't be surprised if Millicent Mayhew enlarged her experience on more than one front. Some of these swarthy guards seem to have made an impression.'

'We're up against a smart lot,' Kenworthy said. 'And to what end?'

'Oh, nobody's told you yet what the asking price was, have they?'

'The public's been led to believe that there was no asking price.'

'And that's what the public must go on thinking. Do you know Franky Tasker?'

'I ought to. I put him away twice.'

'Franky's at present slobbering into his porridge in Cranston Green.'

'What the hell's he doing there?'

'Been a naughty boy in the industrial Midlands.'

'I always told Franky he should never leave the Smoke. He always gets lumbered when he leaves London.'

'The price for the release of the Morley Mortain crowd was that Franky should be allowed to breed white mice in his cell.'

'Now listen, Jack—'

'Straight up, Simon. Anonymous message through an *Express* sports correspondent. Let Franky Tasker keep mice in his cell, and Morley Mortain gets its wives, lovers and bingo-callers back.'

'How did they authenticate it?'

'Mrs Broad's other ear-ring. I might add that the decision to comply was not made overnight.'

'I'll bet it wasn't.'

'The biggest hawk-dove tug-of-war in the life of this Cabinet. We do not give in to terrorists. Give in this once, and every cell in every gaol in the country will be crawling with mice. But in the end, the wets won. You can see why this was kept out of newsprint. Bransby-Lowndes and I were up till the small hours. It coincided with the PM's weekly consultation at the Palace. The buzz is that *She* said, "Oh, let the man have his mice." '

'Franky can't be more than a pawn in all this.'

Forrester looked at Kenworthy pathetically.

'Give us credit for a little *nous*, Simon.'

Kenworthy went to Cranston Green and found Franky Tasker near to tears. He had seen him like that before. Franky was a sentimental soul, especially when he considered himself the victim of injustice—a common event in his life.

'Hullo, Mr Kenworthy. Didn't think you was still with us.'

'I hope you didn't send flowers, Franky.'

'I didn't mean that. Thought you was on the pension.'

'So I am. This is special, Franky. Special for you.'

'Can't you do something for me, Mr Kenworthy?'

'What do you want, Franky? An Alpine rope? Crampons?'

Franky waved his hand towards the farthest corner of his cell. He had thrown one of his blankets over a large cage. Kenworthy lifted it and saw a gleaming modern vivarium, with mirrors, treadmills and clinically hygienic litter. He turned and saw that Franky was cringing.

'Cover it up again, for Christ's sake. They bloody stink. I shall catch something off them. And God knows, some men are bad enough, but the way these little buggers carry on is revolting.'

It appeared that among mice, intercourse follows within seconds of childbirth. Franky explained this in his own words. It seemed to give him extravagant offence.

'Besides, I was in a cell with Micky Maguire and Sammy Hoskins, and we'd the best dummy solo school of any nick I've ever been in. Now they've put me in a one-manner with these perverted little sods, because nobody else would stand for them.'

Franky was actually in the punishment block, this being the only way of concealing from the rest of the prison what concession had been made to him.

'What's it all about, Mr Kenworthy? I've had Spew Hewitson here, and his lips were buttoned like a bishop's gaiters. They seem to think all hell's going to be let loose somewhere, if I don't put up with these bleeders.'

He raised his fist in the direction of the cage.

'Get off her! Get off her! Leave her alone, you fornicating maniac! Cover them up for me, Mr Kenworthy, there's a good 'un.'

Franky was still shrinking back into himself. He did not even want to cross the cell and go near the cage. It was not ham-acting. This was deep-rooted phobia. Whoever had done this to Franky had known how it was going to affect him. Kenworthy put the blanket back into place.

'What are you in for, anyway, this time, Franky?'

'It was all a mistake, Mr Kenworthy.'

'Well, I'm not the one who made it this time, China.'

'They think I had something to do with some furs that got swiped.'

'Caught you wearing one of them, did they?'

'Mr Kenworthy—give me credit! I was down here, see, for this old mate's funeral, and the furs was in one of the cars. Geezer I've never seen in my—'

'Franky, don't tell me you tried to pull the old funeral lark here. Where'd you snarl up the traffic this time? The Bull Ring?'

Franky had once tried this routine in Kilburn, where his luck had been equally rotten. Whereas the average snatch-robber thinks in terms of fast getaways, it had occurred to the resourceful Franky that someone as leisurely as a family mourner is less likely to catch the vigilant eye. Consequently it was with a hearse and a car-load of sad-looking people that he had moved out of Kilburn after a raid on a pavement display. Something like that seemed to have happened this time too—and he had fallen foul, not of fast pursuit with the sirens blaring, but of a simple-minded traffic warden. A hearse, with its professional driver, ought not to drive through red traffic lights. It is even more suspect when followed by a black Austin Princess. The traffic warden was joined by a street patrol already thumbing his aerial—and telling Franky he was nicked. He looked at Kenworthy now with an air of sincere shame.

'And you're not going to do anything to help me, Mr K?'

'Just study your new friends, Franky. You might learn something from them. They don't half-inch one another's coats, for one thing.'

As the screw let Kenworthy out, they heard something violently thrown—a shoe perhaps—against the bars of the cage.

Kenworthy contacted Hewitson—a rendezvous in familiar surroundings. They sat on Edwardian plush at a cast-iron, marble-topped table, partitioned off from others by frosted glass.

'Thought I'd better let you know, Hughie, I'm doubling on your tracks.'

'The Faculty?'

Kenworthy nodded. 'No question of checking up on you, of course.'

'Wouldn't care if you were. Enjoy yourself.'

'Mind if I ask you one thing? This country house: you'll have looked around?'

'Do you think nobody's thought of the obvious since you left?'

It was not clear whether he was resentful or not.

'If the county lads have done a quarter of what we've begged off them, half of them will have qualified as estate agents by now.'

Kenworthy accounted for an inch of Stag bitter. Hewitson was a Newcastle Brown man.

'But you know how it is, Simon. Nobody ever sees anything—and this lot were under stress. One swore it was a gravel drive, another said pebbles. Two said double fronted, two said shallow L-shaped with the door at one side. I asked them all to do me a sketch. Spriggs said he couldn't draw a straight line with a ruler. Mayhew produced three gables, Ogilvy four, Dolly Mason one. Rita Lonsdale gave it a flat roof; she's pregnant again, by the way.'

'That down to Saxby?'

'Or Spriggs. Or one of the Italians. Or Spaniards. Or whoever.'

'Coming back to this house, Hughie—could it have been custom-built for such capers?'

'Could be. But the inside layout isn't necessarily visible from outside. Not one of the party saw what was over the garden wall.'

'Some planning committee must have the records.'

'We'd never get through that lot with the manpower we

have. Mayhew put the building in the 'sixties, and she's the best witness of the bunch. How many years of planning permission does that line up for us? And you know what architects are when it comes to municipal skulduggery. This one probably didn't register his plan—or fiddled it in some way. Or maybe he was a chairman of planners himself.'

'Yes. I know the level we're working at. Is this one of the Manager's jobs? What's your private view, Hughie?'

'That this was a dry run. And if so, they must be feeling very happy at the way it's worked out. Franky's mice must have given someone a big laugh. I think there's some organization—let's say it's the Manager—wanting to make someone part with a lot of money for something big. He's a reluctant client. He needs to be persuaded that the scheme will work. I mean: say they're trying to con some top-class lifer that they can spring him—at a price. Franky's mice prove what can be done. I may be wrong. But I know I'm not wrong about one thing. This is going to happen again. And next time the target won't be a one-man fur-and-feather society in the chokey wing. And if anyone steps out of line, it won't be the Arabian Nights for the hostages.'

'Do you think Saxby tried to step out of line?'

'I don't know. He doesn't seem grievously missed, does he? By the way—' Hewitson finished his drink like a man who had other work to do—'They're letting you have Shiner. Commander, Fraud, is doing his nut. So is Shiner. And—still by the way—what's your cover?'

'Freelance journalism.'

'You'll do no worse than the full-timers. Behave yourself, Simon.'

'I'll try. And if I happen on anything, I'll tell you before I tell Forrester.'

'I know you will. That's why I didn't kick up when I heard you were on it.'

Shiner was the next to meet Kenworthy at the same marble-top.

'You bad old bugger! You have me switched off a case that was going to have me made up to Commissioner, just because you want someone to talk to—'

'It's just that I need your particular brand of respect in the offing, Shiner. How's Fraud?'

'Bloody awful! Two hundred of us, Simon, have been on one case for eighteen months. Multi-national. And as half their UK transactions seem to have been switched through their Rotterdam books, even Inland Revenue doesn't know where the money is. It'll go on another year yet. And then there may not be a case to go forward. And if we think there is, the DPP may not think it will stand up.'

'So you need a change. We'll get a laugh out of Morley Mortain. Do you know anything about the case?'

'Canteen talk.'

Kenworthy told him the Franky Tasker angle, and people in other alcoves turned to look at the hilarity.

'And damned if the fool hadn't tried out in Warwickshire the funeral getaway ploy he got nabbed for in Kilburn.'

'I remember that day,' Shiner said. 'There was a heist from a bank in Swiss Cottage. We never did—'

Then the two looked at each other, and each said 'Hey!' in the same moment.

'Blower, Shiner! Get on to the Midlands. Someone will tell us what else happened that day.'

Shiner had to be rung back. He returned with a glint that reminded Kenworthy of earlier days.

'Wage-snatch at Birmingham Fiveways.'

'And Franky's funeral snarl-up got in the way of the chasers.'

'They hadn't thought of that. They say they think so.'

That was how they came to connect Franky Tasker with the Manager. Hitherto, they'd always thought him too big a fool.

CHAPTER 5

The Manager—sometimes, as is the case with Hoover or Biro, to the delight of the manufacturer, a brand name becomes the public's name for an object. In the case of the Manager, the reverse process had taken place. Organized, managerial crime had thrown up a mythological character. Kenworthy and Wright spoke of one; but they knew he was probably duplicated by rivals. There had been very large-scale, very complex, very clever crimes that had never been wound up. In the 1970s an *ad hoc* Special Crimes squad had been formed to concentrate on activities ascribed to the Manager. They had collated a great deal of very suggestive—and fascinating—information: but very little else.

The Manager remained faceless. It was probable that even his indispensable lieutenants did not know who he was. Special Crimes became certain of two things. The Manager was someone who enjoyed organization for its own sake. His administration, communications and logistics were impeccable. And he was dedicated to crime. The unlawful was where he wanted to function. Obviously, he was in it for gain, but it was possible that he was not a Crœsus. His overall turnover must be astronomic: but so were his overheads. Suppose he were the directing spirit behind the Morley Mortain venture: the ultimate target would have to be monumental, if there was to be much left over the line after he had paid his operatives at rates that would keep them loyal. Clearly he had to remain more than just solvent—but it might be mainly for the action that he was in it. The Morley Mortain business also suggested an impish sense of humour. It was the first time that that had been suspected. It was a promising weakness. Men out for laughs sometimes wanted one at all costs.

Wright delved into CRO and they took a prolonged second look at Franky. The little Cockney had been born in the early 1930s, in an area off the East India Dock Road where survival had depended on fast reactions, speedy withdrawals, and the ability to get up again without much caring that you'd been knocked down. Franky had been a regular figure in Juvenile Courts as soon as he was of an age to appear in them: street-market pilfering, lock-up shops, open counters. More than one presiding magistrate asked him if he had no sense at all. Didn't he ever pause to consider the consequences? The answer, throughout his life, appeared to be No. If he saw something he thought worth pinching, he pinched it: even when, as for example with a consignment of 'Swiss' watches, disposal of the loot was beyond his resources. The time-lapse between the offence and the hand on his shoulder had often been ridiculously short.

He was saved from Borstal by his National Service in the late 1940s, some LCC do-gooder sitting under the Coat of Arms having proclaimed that she thought it might be the making of him. He did not like the army. He lost his head, deserted without an adequate escape-route and ended up in the Glasshouse.

His subsequent civilian career was a familiar pattern of increasing sentences for crimes that were usually senseless—thefts beyond his skills, mates he ought to have known better than to rely on, a cheerful inability to survive the commonest interrogator's dodges.

There were periods of freedom: a year, nine months, two years. It could be that for months at a time he had learned to provide for himself and his dependants without getting caught. It was more likely that somebody was making a staunch effort to keep him straight. Franky married late—at twenty-nine. His wife was a girl he'd been at school with—in the Dallow Road, E.8. The romance of their courtship wasn't on file in CRO.

'I met Lil Tasker a time or two,' Kenworthy said. 'I gave her a quid once, when I was a detective-sergeant and had just got him a lagging. She didn't want to take it—but she was a realist. A sad, uncomplaining woman, who kept his home clean and never went under. You never heard her beef about his damned stupidity. She seemed to take it all as it happened. It must have been true love, Shiner. She must have had a shrewd idea of what she was getting—she'd got it, and that was her walloping-pot. Perhaps there was a time when she thought she could reform him. When she found she couldn't, it was no worse than not winning the pools.'

The Taskers had had a child—latish in life for Lil—a girl Kenworthy remembered seeing when she was about ten, and he was paying the sort of social call that he sometimes did in those days.

'Franky was doing bird for unlawful possession—pocket transistors. Bought them off a chap in a pub, he said. And his daughter was sitting at the table, doing her homework—drawing a map of the routes to the Crusades. I peeped over her shoulder, tried to show interest. She looked up at me with hatred. And yet she was reasonably dressed, well fed. The home had no luxuries, but it was respectable. There ought to be a grade of birthday honour for women like Lil Tasker, who keep life going. The girl had comics, a bashed-up but workable record-player. I've often wondered what became of young Jackie.'

They combed through Franky Tasker's record, hoping to find a turning-point in his activities, a year in which he might have been picked up by someone bigger than himself.

'It's not easy, Shiner. What his form-sheet doesn't tell us is the jobs he got away with. He must have made it sometimes, even Franky.'

Then they found it. 1963: driving a lorry that shed its load. What the hell was Franky doing, driving a lorry? 'Helping a mate out what was took sick,' was what he had told the arresting officer.

'I love it, Shiner, when they talk of a lorry shedding its load. It suggests a will of its own. I sometimes feel that way myself.'

In this case, it was firewood, all over East Acton High Street. They'd done Franky for everything in the book. Insecure load, no HG licence, no Road Fund licence, inefficient silencer, ineffective brakes, uninsured, four bald tyres out of six—and no bulb in his tail-lamp.

'I like the tail-lamp, Shiner. These traffic Wallies make sure it all goes down, once they've licked their pencils.'

This time Franky did not go to gaol, but the fines mounted up.

'And they'd be paid, Shiner. It's a pity somebody didn't ask how. This was a traffic-jam. I am ready to swear, to impede the pursuit of somebody else. To take a squad car in the opposite direction from a crime that was planned. I wonder if this was the first time they'd tried it? How many times did it come off—and none of us spotted it? I dare say we still might find out what else happened in or around East Acton one Thursday morning twenty years ago. Go and get the division to turn over its old incident books. See who gained a few vital minutes while Franky's firewood was causing a tail-back.

'Oh, and Shiner—put out a few discreet enquiries as to what sort of standard of living the Taskers are managing while the bread-nicker's away. I don't want either of us to go—it would draw too much attention. But if—'

But if Franky was under the Manager, his wife wouldn't be lacking. That was one of the significant liabilities that the Manager had to face. Loyalty had to be bought by a better social welfare scheme than the state ran. If mouths were to be kept quiet, then they mustn't get hungry. And men and women did not live out of tins alone. They had to have parity with their neighbours. The network that managed the payments, that assessed needs, that smoothed discontent, had to be vast, secret—and a triumph of efficiency. The Manager, in fact, had to live for efficiency: even if, in his lower ranks, he had to employ men like Franky Tasker.

Shiner's informant reported that there was nothing suspiciously opulent about the Taskers' home. When Lil Tasker went to the supermarket, she shopped with an eye on the pence. And she was still wearing the sort of clothes she had always been satisfied with. They did have TV, but it was a second-hand set, black and white. There was a fridge—five quid 'as found'. No washing-machine, no dishwasher, not even a pedal-bin: garbage in an old metal bucket.

But the daughter was at university. The stack of LP's that she'd left at home had not missed much that had hit the top twenty in the last couple of years.

And the way she dressed, the neighbours said: brown knee-boots, black knee-boots, knee-boots shaggy with nylon fur. Cloak like a patchwork counterpane: well, they don't give these bloody things away, you know.

'Well, couldn't she have worked for them?'

'Work? It's all holidays, isn't it? Goes abroad for three months at a stretch.'

'As I said, Shiner. I've often wondered what became of Jackie Tasker.'

CHAPTER 6

Morley Mortain became almost a Bedfordshire village again. Herbert Spriggs—who had been replaced here and there by menacing substitutes—nudged his way back into the bingo-calling engagements that occupied him six evenings a week. It was rumoured that the Ogilvys were in marital difficulties. The continued closure of the Gospel Hall had not increased the Reverend Yealland's congregation by a single soul. Mrs Commander walked the village street in both ear-rings, and glanced at young men as she had no doubt once eyed the latest ship's company to sign in at Aggie Weston's. Rita Lonsdale went openly by bus to the ante-natal clinic.

Then two events enlivened the newspapers—whose editors had no reason to draw a connection between them.

'You're going to be upset, Simon,' Elspeth said.

'What's this, then?'

She had got hold of the newspaper first at the breakfast table. Kenworthy had heard the BBC news, but nearly cricked his neck, trying to see the headline.

SCOURGE STRIKES NORFOLK VILLAGE

> Yesterday evening, nine members, the entire sitting of the Parish Council of an unassuming community surrounded by beet-fields and sandy pine-forests, were unceremoniously hi-jacked in the sanctity of their monthly meeting, and bundled in waiting transport, away into the unknown.
>
> As happened in a previous incident in the Home Counties, the vicar was ejected from the party before

the carriage of doom moved off, leaving eight families wondering what has struck them.

'Not that,' Elspeth said.

She folded the paper and passed it over. An inquest had been ordered to enquire into the case of a man who had been found hanging in Cranston Green Prison. His name was given as Francis Herbert Morrison Tasker.

'I must get over there,' Kenworthy said.

But Forrester said No. Bransby-Lowndes had put an absolute veto on it.

'Your story is freelance journalism. Your only legitimate point of entry is Norfolk. The local boys are perfectly capable—'

'Is Hewitson going?'

'He's no writ. Forces call less and less for the Met when they can handle things themselves. And the public must not be allowed to make the connection.'

'Cranston Green? There was a case there, wasn't there, a year or two back, of an escape that could only have been engineered by internal collusion? And no progress was made—none of any kind?'

'Other things too, Simon—cot-deaths. And every one accounted for. Every board of enquiry satisfied. If we go running there every time there's an accident, it will look as if we're gunning for them.'

'Jack, I sense a certain similarity between your department and others I've rubbed shoulders with—'

He had to go to Binney St Botolph, the one place where he believed he could be least useful: so much for the omnipotence of the Faculty! The Parish Council was a handful of farmers, a cowman who worked for one of them, a retired corn-chandler's accountant, reputed to be a genius at figures. The Binney St Botolph Council was a self-perpetuating body for which there had been no election for thirty-six years. No one ever put in nomination papers, and all vacancies were filled by co-option. Also among those now in the hands of the Manager was Emily Sturge, village postmistress and Parish Council clerk, who was paid a nominal twelve pounds a year for keeping the minutes, and for forgetting to post the agenda on the village notice-board if ever there was a controversial item on it. The Parish Fathers had been engaged on just such a crucial wrangle at the moment of entry of the Manager's strong-arm men. They were discussing what action to take against a newcomer to Binney who had recently erected without planning permission a light trellis porch about his front door. They had just decided that two of their number should be deputed to walk past that front door and look at it—which they did every day of their lives—so that they could report back at the next meeting. The Binney St Botolph democratic system rarely did anything rash.

Kenworthy knew that it was the Manager who had struck in Binney St Botolph, because he had listened to Radio Norfolk as he drove in along the burgeoning lanes. He had learned that during the night an articulated lorry had jack-knifed across the carriageway on a critical stretch of the A11 just south of Wymondham, jamming a rear wheel in a ditch and holding up traffic in either direction for an hour and a half. The local police were not aware of the relevance of this: how could they be? And such was the influx of journalists into Binney that Kenworthy had to wait to get into the kiosk to phone Shiner. It was some time before anyone but he and Shiner were convinced. The lorry-driver, examined as to how he had managed to jack-knife on an open stretch, maintained that he had overshot a lay-by in which he had intended brewing tea, and had endeavoured to reverse into the further end of it. He was a man without a record. His manner was reported as frank, helpful and apologetic. It could be that he had had a seemingly casual encounter with someone who had offered him a single substantial payment. For the time being, it was obviously going to be very difficult indeed to get him to talk. The articulated was going to get them nowhere. It was one of those little side-plays which the Manager, if not Franky Tasker, had a habit of winning. Kenworthy mused briefly that if Franky had been alive and at liberty, it might well have been he who had driven a twenty-six-wheeler along East Anglia's main artery.

Binney St Botolph was no Morley Mortain. It lacked not only a craft shop, but even street-lighting and sewers, many of its cottages still served by a clanking vehicle that emptied the picturesquely styled night-soil buckets. Until Norwich found a stand-in for Emily Sturge, even the Post Office was closed—and today was Pension Day. The only pub was a tied house owned by a brewer against whom serious ale-drinkers were prejudiced.

The sugar-beet farms stood in glutinous mud. The grocery was packed with women hoping to hear something new. The press, casting prejudice aside, went into the pub as soon as it opened and immersed themselves in a card-game whose significance Kenworthy at first missed. He was aware of animosity when they saw him come in. His freelancing tempted some of them to think of industrial consequences. But he was saved by Barrington Watts of the *Examiner*, who knew him of old (and with whom, in a sense, he had shared Millicent Mayhew). He saw Watts whispering to the others—persuading them perhaps that Kenworthy, if properly handled, might be the key to what was being thought in high places. He drew Kenworthy over with a jerk of his head.

'Want to sit in?'

They appeared to be playing poker without stakes.

'I don't think so,' Kenworthy said. 'Shame to rob you.'

'I'll tell you what it is, Simon.'

Kenworthy had never really adjusted to the contemporary attitude to Christian names: Watts was an impudent sod.

'We've started doing it this way, because in the long run it saves bad blood. We're lining things up for when they come back. We've conceded Emily Sturge to Stuart Morris. Our Editors won't unbuckle the sort of money the *Globe* splashes, so he's bound to get the only woman. Ed Pownall's just won a farmer called Bellamy with two queens, but there are six still in the kitty.'

'That's how you got Millicent Mayhew, is it?'

'On a running flush.'

'I'll be a wild card, thanks.'

Kenworthy drifted away. By late afternoon he was southbound. Nothing was going to be learned in Binney St Botolph until the emigrants were brought back.

The kidnappers made known, through the *Guardian* editorial office, that this time both their demands and the releases would fall into two halves. First, the sum of £50,000 was to be paid to the credit of a Dr Richard Henriques, a Cambridge research medic whose project on chronic cystitis in advanced disseminated sclerosis had been curtailed as part of a series of government economy measures.

Dr Henriques was given a bad time—not only with intrusion on his privacy that was likely to stir up the Press Council—but also by a couple of Hewitson's inspectors. These two, inevitably exposed in the firing line, had Kenworthy's sympathy. They had no choice but to treat Henriques as if he might be involved, and they had little to go on beyond his reactions under pressure. Kenworthy would have liked a look-in himself, but Bransby-Lowndes banned it.

The interrogation was classical: long hours, pouncing on accidental anomalies, bludgeoning accusations, fatigue, confusion, playing on his desire to get back to his family. Henriques was an intelligent man, though at his best only within his specialisms. He was also obstinate, sardonic about the rights of the citizen, obliquely scornful of the police mentality. The final judgement was necessarily subjective. It was a relief to release him from helping with enquiries. The only evidence lay in his responses. No one who talked to him for any length of time could believe that he was bent. He was a clever doctor with a somewhat ingenuous front to everyday living. He was honestly bitter about the way he had been treated by the University Grants people—but he was stunned that anyone should undertake a kidnapping to get him back what he had lost. He went back to Cambridge, where a twenty-four hour tail was put on him. That was a waste of manpower.

This time the country, not just the Cabinet, was split between militancy and appeasement, for this time the demand was made known. What was £50,000, with the welfare of sclerotics temporarily banned from the laboratory? On the other hand, if you gave way now, how much longer was this sort of thing going to go on—and who was going to have to suffer when the line did have to be drawn? The hawks' leader-writers tried to put it in not too crude a way that sooner or later someone was going to have to be sacrificed. And the doves' case was weakened by a general feeling that if the Morley Mortain treatment was going to be repeated, these Norfolk swede-bashers had been driven off to have a damned good time, anyway.

The government made adamant statements. There was to be no giving way. (There was no admission that they had given way last time.) There was no alternative. These people must be shown that they could not get away with it. Only one columnist listed the other projects that would have, in all equity, to be restored if the authorities gave in now. It would cost two and a half million, and would include an enquiry into the quiescence of Ströhm's bacillus at sub-arctic temperatures, the anticipation of antibiotics in a sixteenth-century herbal, and the retention of radio-activity in a Nevada cactus.

Kenworthy, Forrester and Bransby-Lowndes considered the hypothesis that the Manager was a man of social conscience; even that this was some new Manager, *débutant* on the scene, who had hit upon an ingenious device for frustrating government policy. They briefly rejected the angle. Tasker's mice had been a nasty little joke. Henriques' research was an appetising irrelevance, served up before the Borgian main course that was still to come. Something startling was going to emerge in the second half of the demand.

Government did not drag its feet: it stood still. And the public was lulled by non-event into supposing that nothing so very drastic would happen in the end. But the Manager showed less patience than he had done with his guests from Bedfordshire. In the second week of the Norfolkmen's exile, another pair of ear-rings was delivered through the post to a disturbed spouse. They differed from those returned to Commander Broad in that this pair—scarcely more than blobs of red plastic—were without value, even ornamental. But one of them did have an ear attached. And since they were Emily Sturge's adornments, it was assumed that it was Emily Sturge's ear. Forensic science could not accept this premise, lacking primary evidence, and was able neither to advance nor retard anyone's file. In the eyes of most people, however, an ear was an ear, no matter whose, and England was shocked.

No politician had the courage to argue—at least not in public—that an ear is not exactly a fatal organ to lose. The Norfolk lobby had strong support. No farmer's wife wondered which of her husband's appendages might shortly be committed to the mails, but there may have been some anxious fantasies.

Mr Speaker rejected a request by Mr Christopher Medlock, MP, for an emergency debate, and the Home Secretary won some applause for the indignation with which he deplored the callousness of this act of surgery. Then an adviser from some anonymous pool of inner strategical strength had the good fortune to discover that it was simply not true that Dr Henriques' researches had been cut off. No final decision had been reached in the case—and this went too for Ströhm's bacillus, the antibiotic herbal and Nevadan cacti. Press reports had misinterpreted unauthorized remarks by a junior official. (The Faculty was asked to look into the state of security in the University Grants Committee's office.) Three days later, grants totalling two and a half million pounds were not restored—they had never been suppressed—they were ratified. And the first half of the party—three farmers and a corn-chandler's accountant—were deposited at various points within six miles of Binney St Botolph. The story that they had to tell evoked neither Turkish harems nor luxury service-flats. The premises in which they had been confined appeared indeed to have been constructed round the rose-garden court of a country villa, but it was a sorry tale now of bedboards and biscuit mattresses, of strong lamps kept burning all night, and of an inadequate daily intake of calories, served up in unpalatable gruels. Those who returned made it clear that they did not envy the lot of those that remained; especially not of the postmistress.

CHAPTER 7

Meanwhile, events had continued to unfold on the second front of the Manager's activities. The coroner's court had been satisfied that Franky Tasker had taken his own life by hanging himself by his prison braces from the framework of his prison bedcot, which he had stood up on end for the purpose. Unable to contrive an adequate drop, his death was due to strangulation, the initial stages of which must have demanded a remarkable willpower. Evidence was heard from prison staff and one inmate, Micky Maguire, that Tasker had shown signs of depression of late. He seemed to be adapting himself to confinement with less than his customary resignation. Asking why he had recently been transferred to the punishment block, the coroner was told that this was the only way in which the Governor could satisfy the prisoner's repeated requests for solitude: he was in no way subject to punishment routines. It was felt that, over a short period, the opportunity for unharassed reflection might help him. No: his condition had not been considered sufficiently serious for hospitalization. There was no reference to mice. Kenworthy could not resist the conclusion that everything possible had been done to keep the issues in front of the coroner as uncomplicated as possible. No: it was considered undiplomatic for Kenworthy to pay another visit to Cranston Green at the moment, but it was agreed to provide him with photocopies of all the coroner's officer's files, including the path report.

Then, one day during the first stage of the Binney St Botolph affair, he came home from the Faculty office to learn that he had had a visitor.

'And perhaps it is as well you were out,' Elspeth said. 'I think that the pair of you might not have got on too well together.'

'Oh? Who?'

'She is a young lady with a certain sartorial nonchalance. You might have drawn reactionary conclusions.'

'Do tell me.'

'Or put it another way. I've often wondered what I would wear if I had to call on a policeman whom I had detested for years, to complain that he was a party to murdering my father. Now I know. I'd put on Alpine green tights under sandals, a poncho with zigzag stripes in orange and heliotrope, a yellow floral bandanna and an extremely expensive and nearly new suede sombrero.'

'Jackie Tasker.'

'I put in some groundwork for you, Simon. She's calling again this evening, and there's now a possibility that she might listen to what you say. For a time, anyway. She dislikes you very much indeed.'

'I remember getting a dirty look from her when she was ten.'

'She's gathered strength since then.'

'How old is she now?'

'Twenty-two. Last Tuesday.'

'You did cover some fundamentals, didn't you?'

'It was the only way,' Elspeth said.

Jackie came as the early evening reached the coffee stage. She was unrecognizable either from Elspeth's description or from the night of her homework on the Crusades. Her hair, dark chestnut, of which she had rather a lot, had been combed out to the right-hand side, where it fell out in a broken-ended cascade from under a brimless, straw-coloured cloche hat. The left-hand side of the hair over her scalp had been drawn so tight that the shape of her skull was plainly visible: an almost perfectly spherical skull, and rather a small one for such abundant hair, Kenworthy thought. She had on a knee-length yellow dress so cut as to cancel out any bosom she might have possessed. He remembered one of his aunts wearing a dress like that at a picnic on Box Hill when he was about seven. Her shoes were in silver brocade and would have been suitable for dancing the Charleston or the Black Bottom.

'I can see you are looking at me,' she said without humour.

'Every woman to her taste—or to the taste of her friends.'

'There's no need to be like that. One just doesn't want to be conspicuous.'

'Of course not. I'm often aware of curious eyes on me in a crowd.'

'Sarcastic sod! Don't you know there's a set going about these days aping the 'twenties? I'm mixing. I'm doing metropolitan sub-cultures for my thesis.'

'Yes. I heard you were at university. Social studies?'

'Criminology.'

She said it with a knife-stab of finality—a challenge to him to find out more—and a strong hint that he wouldn't.

'And now if we're through with the civilities, can we get down to business? I'm told you're a good family man, Mr Kenworthy. I knew I'd hear someone speak well of you, if I lived long enough.'

'You've only been with us twenty-two years, Miss Tasker.'

'Don't be smart. I want to know why none of you were at my father's inquest.'

'I think the people involved were all there, weren't they?'

'No one at all from the London end.'

'I don't see how anyone from London could have helped.'

'If you people hadn't gone sticking your noses in, he'd still be alive, Mr Kenworthy. You went to Cranston Green to interview him.'

'There was no hint then of future suicide.'

'There was no suicide. And you were behind some scurrilous enquiries here at home. How old's our fridge? What size television screen? You even had my LP's turned over.'

So somebody had done that job unsubtly: some men had finesse, others saw all problems as a frontal assault.

'I am trying not to be hysterical. I loved my father, Mr Kenworthy.'

'I had a certain liking for him, too. And I always greatly admired your mother. But you can't say he always made the best use of the brains God gave him.'

'Neither do you. All my life I've believed in you as a rotter, Mr Kenworthy. Now I know that's not true. You're just plain bloody stupid.'

'Well—that's settled that,' he said.

'Because my father had to be got out of the way, when attention of a certain kind was drawn to him.'

'At a certain stage in certain other events, do you mean?'

She looked at him sharply.

'What events are you thinking of?'

'Morley Mortain? Binney St Botolph?'

'You see a connection? You have a funny way of setting about things.'

'Not going to your father's inquest was part of that funny process. That *would* have been stupid. I take it you were there?'

'And it stank.'

'Of mice?'

She looked at him blackly.

'If that's some sort of joke, it's about the worst taste since Lord Chief Justice Goddard made one about *Swing, swing together.*'

So even she did not know about the mice. And that could be. Franky had had no recent visits, and any mail from him would still be dodging about in a Midlands CID office.

'My father hated mice. He was scared of them as any old woman sweeping out a cupboard. He got it off his silly mother, when he was a kid. But what *is* this about mice?'

'I'll come back to it. Tell me what did stink.'

'The English way of covering things up,' she said. 'Like

when a drunk dies in custody—or there's been rough stuff in a nick after a demonstration.'

'Neither happened in this case.'

'I know that. Are you going to listen to me—or are you playing the *esprit de corps* game too?'

'I'd like to listen.'

'Well, listen to this for a start. I'm getting a private pathologist's report on my father. The coroner has given clearance for burial. We're dragging our feet about the funeral.'

'And what do you hope to find? Or should I say expect?'

He was evolving respect for this young lady. He had always had a soft spot for sergeants who talked to him as she did.

'Why should I play everything into your hands?'

'Because there are moments when men like me have to make a decision. I've just made one. By the time you leave here this evening, I shall have told you everything that's on my mind. You and I can shadow-box—or we can each take the chance that the other's straight. And if I'm wrong about you, I've more to lose than you have, Miss Tasker.'

'Jackie.'

'I answer to Simon.'

He did not care to turn to see the look on his wife's face.

'The official path report spoke of bruises about the shoulders and ribs, consequent on his banging against the woodwork of the bed. The doctor was as coy as you might expect about it, but he said that Dad might have had second thoughts when he started to asphyxiate. He could have made matters worse by trying to free himself. But I know it wasn't that sort of struggle. You'd have to fight to hang a man by his braces in a confined space. I know what my pathologist will find.'

'Let's hope he goes into it with an open mind—which is more than you have.'

'Isn't it obvious? Dad would never have killed himself. He was always hare-brained cheerful. Last time I saw him in court, he looked as happy as an imbecile when his brief started the weariest plea in mitigation I've ever heard in my life. Look, Simon—there's a locked-room mystery here. Why was no other prisoner on the landing not asked whether he'd heard any scuffle?'

'Did you ask the coroner that?'

'I did. He brought a Detective Chief inspector back and asked him. Oh—they went through all the forms. He said that had been gone into—there was nothing.'

'Scuffling and shouting are not unknown in the chokey wing, anyway.'

'They stick together, don't they? What were you saying about mice?'

Kenworthy told her, retaining nothing.

'The bastard!' she said. 'And before you ask me who I'm talking about: I haven't the foggiest idea.'

'You mean you don't know the man your father often worked for—and who's been so kind to your interests while he's been away?'

'That man hasn't survived by advertising himself.'

'But you never had a conscience about touching the money that came to you? I know I wouldn't—'

'Why should I? My mother paid a price for it, if Dad didn't.'

'How do you receive it? There must be an agent.'

'There isn't. At least, he never makes contact. I have a bank account. Payments into it are cash deposits, never at my own branch.'

'And you opted for criminology. Defensive or offensive?'

'Neither. Pure science. A desire to understand. Now I must rush. I've got a date on Streatham Common with a couple who look roughly as I do.'

'Before you go. This phobia of your father's about mice—it went deep?'

'He couldn't stand them. He could do nothing about it.'

'Might he have hanged himself to be rid of them?'

'Not that,' she said. 'No—not Dad—'

But he could see that she was miserably uncertain.

There was no other development until the Manager made known his terms for the release of the remaining East Anglians. It was that a named prisoner should be transferred from a crowded urban gaol in the West Riding to the Open Prison at Grendon Underwood, Bucks.

CHAPTER 8

Kenworthy and Wright demanded a copy of the Grendon Underwood nominal roll. Wright went down the names with more gleams of recognition than Kenworthy did. Professionally, he was nearer to this crop. There were two who brought him special joy.

'You know, Simon, the way a certain type gravitates to the cushy numbers—it's an admission that we look on some crimes as not specially shameful. I've come across it again and again: corruption, conversion, local government fiddles—they all end up in no time in the easy joints.'

'I suppose white collar crooks know how to behave themselves—and won't make a break for it.'

'Here's one who won't, anyway. When they move him from Yorkshire to Grendon, we'll have somebody taking notes every time he turns over in bed.'

The Manager's new friend was William Greenlees Waterlow, and his downfall had coincided almost to the month in which his name would have graced the larger print of a Birthday Honours List. The Central Chancery of the Orders of Knighthood had been informed of the colour of the enquiry that was afoot and was saved with only a day or two to spare from posting their five-week notice letter. It had all started when the Burgesses, a married couple promoting themselves to their second home, submitted plans that had been drawn up for them in his private time by an architect with whom Eric Burgess had been at grammar school. In the County Offices he was quietly told — at clerical level at an outer counter — that fifty pounds would greatly help his application through the works. He had demurred.

'Have it your own way. We're getting on into June. The Committee doesn't meet in August. If you don't want shunting over into September, maybe till well into the autumn — '

Burgess had still refused to pay. His architect friend had shrugged his shoulders.

'You won't miss fifty quid. Put in a complaint, and you'll not have a shred of proof. The conversation didn't happen. Your papers will go to the bottom of the pile. It's happening all along the line. This authority has 80,000 applications outstanding at the present time.'

But Burgess went to the police and got as far as a detective-sergeant, who told him that no case could be brought on the existing evidence. And Burgess's application was not delayed, because the counter-clerk, somewhat green at the arts of corruption, took fright and thought he had better show a clean nose.

But the detective-sergeant dug out three other applicants and found that they had all quietly complied. They wanted no fuss made. It was a small price they had paid. You had to allow for it nowadays. It was happening all along the line.

A trap was laid and the clerk fell into it. He wept. His career was gone. His home was broken. He was a feeble criminal who hadn't been trying more than a few months. What he'd gained financially had not made up for loss of sleep.

'It isn't fair, Sergeant. All right—I've had fifty pounds here and there. What about the big boys? It goes into hundreds of thousands when William Waterlow's organizing a site on the Poplars Industrial Estate. Ask him what he had from Peterson and Bold for keeping Ashmore-Perkins out of Upper Kealey.'

Ashmore-Perkins: used-car dealers. The site was worth recurring millions. No immediate action was taken. Waterlow was a County Councillor, had Planning and Development in the palm of his hand. It was dangerous even to contemplate him: till he got caught in the cross-fire of someone else's battle.

An electronic components factory had won a site at Cross Winds. Waterlow had favoured the allocation. Then he came along with a friendly request: insure with United Industrial, and he and the Company Secretary would split the commission. The Company Secretary did not want to play, and Waterlow produced a pollution headache that would have sent the firm beyond their bankers' limits. What Waterlow did not know was that a bigger insurance battle had been fought and won. National Preferential concluded that they wanted him off their pitch. Evidence against him started being put under the noses of senior officers. It happened sometimes along the line. After a very long trial, Waterlow went down on a very long charge-sheet.

And now he was being put up for a new club. Grendon Underwood. No great victory, perhaps. He was just about due for Open Prison. It wouldn't, in the normal course, have been Grendon. So what was so special about Grendon?

Shiner thought he knew. He had a vivid memory for names he had come across in the Fraud Squad. Samuel Scales and Walter Ulliatt. Scales had been insurance and Ulliatt had been used cars. Waterlow, Scales and Ulliatt were on their last lap towards freedom. What more useful than a little cosy committee-work under a regime of Her

Majesty's less rigorous hospitality? Either it suited the Manager for Waterlow, Ulliatt and Scales to get together for their forward planning; or they had paid heavily for his services, impressed by the demonstration case of Morley Mortain.

CHAPTER 9

It happened around this time that Kenworthy sat on a symposium at the London Crime Writers' Association's monthly Club Night. There was a good turn-out: Dick Francis looking as if he were on his way to a dinner. Every time he saw Dick Francis, he looked as if he were on his way to a dinner. Desmond Bagley arguing the toss. Margaret Yorke, always eager for new ploys for Inspector Grant. Harry Keating, his beard a little too black and too full to qualify him visually as a *guru*. Did he lie on a bed of nails to write his *Times* book-reviews?

Not a bad lot, Kenworthy thought. They tried. They talked to their GPs about establishing times of death. They rang up police PROs to find out when they ought to retire their stock inspectors. The only ones he mistrusted were those of the women who were keenly awaiting the authoritative announcement that the mantle of Agatha Christie had fallen on their shoulders.

Towards a Philosophy of Crime—that was the portentous core of the evening. Kenworthy, the lightest weight on the panel, was put in to bat first. He had not thought much about it, realized when he looked out at the attentive faces, that he had not thought about it enough: he had no epigrams ready, no prepared juicy examples. Feeling prosaic, he began to tap off his categories on his fingertips.

'Domestic—casual—opportunist—professional small-time—professional big-time—white collar—'

'What's a white collar crime?' someone asked.

'Company books, expense accounts, staff timesheets. Then above that – I'm thinking in terms of a definite progression – we have organized crime. I've got into the habit of calling it managerial.'

He was aware that beside him, Maxwell Durren must be looking bored. Durren always did look bored when it was a policeman who had the right to hold forth. Durren, now in his late forties, still succeeded in radiating something of the aura of a juvenile lead. It was hard to pin down: as if he had somehow preserved the superciliousness of youth. Durren was crime correspondent of one of the more self-conscious of the Sundays. Not for him Rita Lonsdale, Millicent Mayhew and Emily Sturge. He was ahead of that field, had got there by presenting theories as facts, was almost always at cross-currents with the Establishment, was a master of sparkling and meretricious paradox. But he was always well informed about personalities and movements. Durren had an expense account that enabled him to pay his informants at a better rate than the Met could; and when they talked to him, they did not feel that they were grassing. On the rare occasions when Kenworthy had gone to him for help, it had been conceitedly given, with a double show of reluctance and self-congratulation.

'I'd go a stage further and say there's a crime higher than I'd put managerial. I'm thinking of the man who gets away with something that isn't made a crime until after he's cleaned up on it.'

'For example?'

That was Christopher Medlock, on Kenworthy's other hand, another non-friend.

'I was thinking for example of the man who discovers a loophole in the Exchange Control Regulations. And it isn't plugged until he's made his packet. He hasn't committed any crime – but now they've got to make it one.'

'Exchange Control has been lifted,' Durren muttered: self-satisfied sod. Kenworthy had often wondered whether Durren's income—the Bentley that he kept alongside his yacht at Antibes, his hospitality on Tenerife—was entirely derived from the top rung of journalism. He was far from projecting Durren as the Manager. He did not think that Durren had ever committed a crime in his life. But as a source of intelligence to the top-liners, he would surely be unmatched. Durren had a consummate knowledge of what even the Manager needed to know.

'I think there may be some people here tonight who know what I mean,' Kenworthy said sourly.

'You talk of progression in crime as if it's more admirable at the top,' someone said from the audience. 'What's the moral difference between your casual opportunist and your top managerial?'

'Ethically, perhaps, none at all. But there's a difference in technique—in self-control. And that's where I draw a line across the board.'

'Meaning ruthlessness?'

'Not only. Your common criminal—I'm sorry if I seem a snob—is more riddled with superstition than any walk of life I know. And I'm not excluding the theatre. It's been a godsend to me, many a time, the man who leaves his visiting-card. I don't mean he carries a rabbit's foot. He has to do things always the same way—the way it worked last time—his rites and rituals—his preambles—perhaps a drink in the same bar before he sets out, or after he's finished. A man who breaks in through walls always goes through the wall. A man who comes up through the floorboards only knows his way in through the floor.'

Kenworthy felt as if he were failing to put it across.

'Eighty-plus per cent of villains have a trademark that they wouldn't leave if they had the tiniest showing of sense. But above my double line, they know better. The

Manager isn't superstitious. He doesn't repeat himself.'

'Surely—'

But the chairman wanted to press on with the other main speakers. Durren produced a few sniggers, mostly from in-jokes that people wanted to show they understood. The last to speak was Christopher Medlock, who got no laughs at all. He was not a laughing man. He did not see crime—or anything else, apparently—as a laughing matter.

Medlock was an MP, a perpetual backbencher. Though he rarely appeared in court himself these days, he was a criminals' solicitor, and in the House the criminals' mouthpiece and guardian. He specialized in prisoners' rights. Free-vote opposition to capital punishment had members from both sides listening to him. His eye for anything redolent of the police-state was never asleep. On prison reform, as on CS gas and plastic bullets, he was repetitive and immovable. But one sometimes wondered if he respected anyone who was not a criminal. His father had been a recidivist. That was where it had all started. His first legal practice had been low-level, police court stuff. Medlock had helped many a casual opportunist through a loophole that had later had to be stopped.

'I disagree with practically all of what both speakers have said—'

The set-piece talks were all pretty dull. It was during question time that the session limbered up. Someone asked—the entire meeting had been waiting for it—about Morley Mortain and Binney St Botolph.

'Has the panel a solution to this mystery?'

A grand laugh. Crime Writers rushed in where angels tended to watch it.

'I'd prefer to leave that to the professionals.'

Maxwell Durren glanced it straight over to Kenworthy.

'I'm a bit removed from the action nowadays,' Kenworthy said, hoping to goodness that it was not general knowledge that he was helping the Faculty. Durren and

Medlock would know, of course.

'I'd be interested to know how long our legislators are prepared to go on giving way,' he said, throwing it hard over to Medlock.

And Medlock threw a bomb.

'To me the most interesting point is why the powers-that-be allowed Franky Tasker to die.'

There was slightly stunned confusion. The Tasker connection had been suppressed. One did not float indiscretions in front of the Crime Writers: one only pretended to. Christopher Medlock had surely boobed. That was always a danger for a man playing multiple roles; but Medlock had had as much practice at that as any man in public life. He tried to pick himself up in his next sentence.

'I've heard it said there's a connection. I just wonder what people think.'

'New angle to me,' Durren said. It wouldn't be, of course, but maybe he did not want to pre-empt his next weekend's revelations.

'And me,' Kenworthy said.

The meeting was temporarily stuck. But in this bunch there was always someone minded to save the situation.

'Would you say, Mr Kenworthy, that the Morley Mortain case proves your previous point – that your top criminal does not repeat himself? Or has he at Binney St Botolph?'

Kenworthy hesitated. A vital sequence was being played out – a gambit. Medlock had lost a valuable piece: perhaps he had given it away. Perhaps the lapse about Franky had been an attempt to pick up information carelessly dropped. Kenworthy wasn't going to give any away.

'Surely,' someone contributed, 'he's repeated himself already. Throwing the vicar out. Shocking us with earrings and ears. They're repetition.'

'That's not what I meant,' Kenworthy said. 'Those are not superstitions. Those are repetitions for repetition's sake. I was referring to involuntary repetition.'

The questioner sat back, considerably less than half satisfied, whispered something to his neighbour.

'And there haven't been involuntary repetitions in these two cases?'

This was Medlock again, leaning forward.

'How do I know? I just read what's in the papers. You'd better ask Chief Super Hewitson.'

After the meeting, Christopher Medlock isolated Kenworthy—not difficult, since Durren was anxious to be away. They went to the Old King Lud. Medlock was barely a drinker, but he played with a half-pint of mild.

'You hesitated, Kenworthy, when I bowled you the googly—the one about repeating himself.'

'I was still getting over your gaffe—about Frank Tasker.'

'That wasn't a gaffe. It was a try-out. I'm raising it in the House tomorrow.'

Medlock was the scourge of Home Secretaries.

'To come back to my point—'

Medlock could not conceal his real anxiety to know. Medlock would know that Kenworthy was part-timing with Forrester; he had a way of knowing anything with which he might one day embarrass someone. Medlock was an enemy of the Faculty, as he was of any police department that he did not consider properly accountable.

'You're wondering why I'm so eager to know?'

'It certainly seems to matter to you.'

'Of course it matters to me. If it could happen to Tasker, it could happen to others. Besides, I rather liked Tasker.'

'So did I, in a way.'

'So: involuntary repetition? Trademark, Mr Kenworthy?'

'Franky came to you when he was in trouble, did he?'

'Always.'

'Who paid his brief?'

'There was a standing kitty. You must know that.'

'I've known there had to be. You're telling me that's all you know?'

'That's all I could afford to know,' Medlock said. 'You understand that very well. A solicitor is an officer of the court.'

And by virtue of the position that he had carved for himself, Medlock must be beyond criticism, beyond even rumour. There were too many waiting to catch him out. Kenworthy went on pressing his point.

'A sort of common insurance policy?'

'You could call it that. A very good term for it.'

An insurance policy that was part of the Manager's welfare state—

'But you're stalling, Kenworthy. Don't change the subject. You're not answering my question. Involuntary repetition—?'

'I'm honestly not aware of any.'

Medlock studied Kenworthy with an expression that mixed disbelief with contempt. Kenworthy was determined to give the man nothing.

'I repeat: I have clients who are wondering whether their turn will come next.'

'Then let them ask for police protection.'

'You know that's a silly answer.'

'Let the police know who they are. Hewitson and his team need every pointer they can get.'

'I cannot believe you know so little about confidences betwen solicitor and client.'

Medlock knew now that he was going to get no more. He also knew that there was something to be got. He made ready to go without bothering to finish his drink.

Kenworthy remained alone and had another, picked

up someone's abandoned evening paper. The editorial was crying for William Waterlow to be moved. Emily Sturge's ear had won that day.

CHAPTER 10

The Home Secretary delayed for several days, though no one now seriously believed that he would abandon the rest of the Norfolk party. It was as if he knew he was going to be forced, but did not mean to be rushed.

One outcome of this was the delivery through Binney St Botolph Post Office of a second well-sealed packet, identical to the first, and loathsomely presumed to contain Emily Sturge's other ear. It actually held a small cardboard box, ideal for the transport of an ear: but no ear. There was only the small round blob of red plastic that had enhanced its lobe. This was the final warning.

Mr Christopher Medlock put down a private notice question to the Home Secretary. Would his Right Honourable Friend make a statement of his intentions in what was now popularly known as the case of Emily's ear?

HER MAJESTY'S PRINCIPAL SECRETARY OF STATE FOR HOME AFFAIRS:	I am grateful to my Honourable Friend for the opportunity to clarify this painful issue. (*Laughter.*) I see nothing to laugh at. (*Interruption*: You've still got both ears.)
MR SPEAKER:	Order!
THE HOME SECRETARY:	I am sorry that Honourable Members opposite see this as a joke. I was about to say that after very much heart-

searching, Her Majesty's Government has decided, out of common humanity, to comply with the fairly trivial request put forward by those who are holding a group of Her Majesty's subjects in quite unacceptable detention.

AN OPPOSITION MEMBER: Where has the Government's sense of common humanity been this last couple of weeks? Why was this decision not taken days ago?

THE HOME SECRETARY: It is not as easy as that. These things are never easy. You cannot make complex arrangements at the touch of a button. (*Cries of* Why not?)

A MEMBER: What is so complex about moving one man a hundred and twenty miles?

THE HOME SECRETARY: It shall be done, sir. (*Loud Government cheers.*)

By now, the cardboard box that had not contained an ear, had been examined in laboratories. It yielded no prints, but the report did mention that the box was of a type widely used by the dental profession for sending impressions and dentures through the post.

'This is the second time we've come across a dentist,' Kenworthy said. 'Was it Rita Lonsdale, in the first batch, who had to have treatment—and declared herself well looked after?'

Bransby-Lowndes, a man of refinement, shuddered.

'You're not suggesting that that poor woman's ear was removed by a dentist?'

★

The Manager kept his word.

The citizenry of Binney St Botolph was restored to its full establishment and the experience of one of them may be taken as representative.

Joseph Arthur Ketteringham was an arable farmer who had effectively not been out of Binney St Botolph in his life. To say this is to ignore the annual package deal on which his wife insisted, and which had taken him on various charter flights to various places where the tea and the beer were defective. Except for a certain flexibility in his Income Tax and VAT returns (*They know we all do it. A man would be a fool not to*) he was an honest citizen and a bulwark in the parish against any ill sniff of change. If he had had to crystallize himself into a slogan, it would have been 'Stand still with Ketteringham.'

He had not enjoyed being kidnapped. He had not enjoyed being transplanted from his farm, detached from the wife whom he loved so familiarly that conversation between them had become superfluous. When Joe Ketteringham went to bed at night, it was like a well-rehearsed if pedestrian ballet. His left foot came down on the same corner of bedroom carpet as he eased the leg of his long-johns down over his right knee.

Under the Manager's administration he had been put into a single bed so narrow that he was afraid to do anything in it except lie on his back. He lay awake for a long proportion of the first night. Shortly after sleep did creep up on him—and at a moment when he would gladly have turned over to sleep for ever—a voice over a loudspeaker told him that day had begun, and that he was to pay close attention to the instructions that he was about to be given. He was to get out of bed, wash, shave and dress within the next five minutes with materials that he would find by the washbasin, then stand on the left of his door with his back to the wall. Ketteringham's counter to any unacceptable personal attack had always been strictly negative. Metaphorically, in adversity he stood still. In this case, he lay still. And this reaction felt so satisfyingly successful that his eyes closed and he drifted away into a confused dream about the tax-deductible proportion of a new combine beet-harvester. The throwing open of his door brought him back coldly to reality. The sheets were pulled from him and two men, foreigners, were raising him to his feet. Ketteringham had met foreigners abroad, where they belonged, though he found them scarcely less forgivable for that. These two were swarthy, which put them in an ethnic subgenus. And when they spoke to him in English, it was without a true grasp of idiom, which underlined their effrontery.

'To your feet! Do as one is told!'

'Take your hands off me!'

Whereupon a hand bunched into a fist landed in his diaphragm with the follow-through judged by a man of experience. When he was able to straighten himself up again, the Arab—or Spaniard or Gypsy—held himself poised to bring his knuckles down over Ketteringham's mouth.

'You dress. You make bed. You stand by door, back to wall.'

He stood there a long time, until finally—it must have been after half an hour—the movement of wheels along a corridor suggested the approach of a trolley. They had been offered nothing to eat since their arrival. Breakfast had the consistency and pigmentation of porridge, but whatever meal had been used smelled suspiciously of inferior animal feed.

All ensuing meals were equally obnoxious, and they were so irregular that, with the windows never unshuttered, the passage of time was incalculable. There was no contact with other members of the group. The room was naked of anything with which a man might occupy himself. There were no books, no radio other than the centrally fed speaker, which came on only for peremptory announcements. There was a house-telephone on the wall, but its line was dead. Ketteringham was not told when the first half of the party was released. When his own release was abruptly announced, the news had about it no reality.

They were shepherded along the corridors and down the stairs, prodded with gun-butts like sheep being driven into a dip. They passed through a hall: Ketteringham seemed to remember an oil-painting of stormy waves breaking on a shore. But the Manager's henchmen treated any sign of curiosity with vicious little jabs in the small of the back. There was no loitering. The van—black, dark blue?—was pulled up close to the front door, its back open. It was drizzling. Ketteringham was last aboard. He and his fellow Councillors had not caught sight of each other since their arrival here. How long ago had that been? Two weeks? A month? The time-confusion technique had worked. Ketteringham was worried about what he would find undone on his farm. He was twisted sick about a contract for aerial crop-spraying that he ought to have renewed.

And then, in the van, that damned woman from the Post Office talked. Mrs Sturge's tongue could not be stilled. It made up now, on the cross-country drive, for her long days without a listener. Something about having her ear cut off. Squit and nonsense! Why should anybody want to cut anybody else's ear off? Even in mid-torrent of all that had recently happened to him, Joe Ketteringham jibbed at accepting the unusual.

But Emily Sturge was patting a dressing that was plastered on under a chunk of hair at the side.

'Have I got to take the bandage off to prove it?'

For the second time they were driven in a way that made it impossible to guess time, distance or route. Then they were made to alight singly, a mile or two away from each other. Ketteringham was put down in a lane four miles from his home. He tried to see by the cloud-filtered moonlight what state Thomas Loynes's beet-tops were in; he'd thought his own were beginning to yellow dangerously just before the abduction.

Ketteringham eventually got home, noticed as soon as he put his foot in his yard that somebody had been at things: had brought a ladder from the old coach-house and left it out. Although it was the small hours of the night, the kitchen light was on. His wife was waiting up for him. Hewitson, assuming that the Manager would keep his bargain, was on hand to go into action with a hand-picked team.

He had also had road-blocks out to stop any vehicle that might be carrying concealed passengers. But the fleet of cars at his disposal was limited. The countryside was interlaced with a network of minor roads. And the Manager did not trip up over details; it was not beyond him to be in touch with the driver of his van by radio, telling him where to get off the clearways.

Hewitson's priority target was Emily Sturge. He talked to her himself, as soon as she had been looked at in the Norfolk and Norwich Hospital.

'I take it he used antibiotics?' the examining doctor asked her.

'I don't know what he used. He did ask me if I was allergic to penicillin.'

'Well. There's no sign of any infection. And with plastic surgery—'

'Never mind about plastic surgery. The nurse has promised me a boiled egg. All these weeks I've kept thinking of a boiled egg.'

Hewitson wanted a description of the man who had done the mutilation. But he had not set his hopes realistically. Mrs Sturge would have been heavily sedated in advance. All she could say was that he was a young man—well, not old. Thinning hair, brushed back; rimless glasses. And he hadn't worn a white coat. She'd have thought a doctor would have worn a white coat for a job like that. The omission seemed to distress her almost as much as the act of surgery itself. Of course, she had not known at first that he was a doctor. They hadn't said—hadn't told her what they were going to do. The first thing she knew, she was being given an injection. It was only afterwards—

'Are you sure it was a doctor? Could it by any chance, do you think, have been a dentist?'

Emily Sturge was more annoyed than surprised by that notion. She looked at Hewitson as if she thought there must be something wrong with his basic intelligence.

'You wouldn't go to a dentist for a job like that, now, would you?'

'I wouldn't go to anyone for a job like that,' Hewitson said, hoping that that was not striking too frivolous a note.

'You'd go to a dentist for anything to do with your teeth,' Emily Sturge informed him, establishing her own sanity, if doubting his.

Meanwhile, the cheque-book journalists were waiting for the opening of the traps. Ed Pownall of the *Sunday Herald* had won Joe Ketteringham with a flush of spades.

Some of the papers did not quite know what to make of the contrast in the way that Morley Mortain and Binney St Botolph had been treated. But Kenworthy understood it.

'First he shows he can spend lavishly and persuade. Then he shows that he can get tough and maim. The big one's still to come.'

The Kenworthys had another visit from Jackie Tasker—this time in pure and punctilious punk: hair in close-cropped contrasting strips of orange and green, eyes mascaraed to the point at which it was painful to look at them. Again, Kenworthy had the impression of a small, very globular cranium. She must have had her scalp shaved to accommodate her battery of wigs.

'Have you been to Cranston Green yet?' she asked.

'Not yet.'

'Why not?'

Kenworthy told himself that she was under strain. He was patient.

'It isn't deemed politic that I should go to Cranston Green at present.'

'Don't give me that. You can go anywhere you like.'

'Not so, young lady. You don't know what protocol is.'

'I know where it gets you—nowhere fast. And that goes for the medical profession, too. They stick together, those boys.'

'It sometimes looks that way.'

'Simon—'

She leaned forward and grasped his knee. In the punk guise, her face looked thin-featured and mean.

'Simon, I *know* that there are injuries on my father's body that show that he was executed.'

'And your pet pathologist won't oblige you by saying so?'

'All he'll say is that it might be that way.'

That was probably as far as he could legitimately go. How often had Kenworthy looked at evidence, known what it meant—and known that it would be a waste of time bringing it to court? But he thought better of trying to reason that out with Jackie Tasker at the moment. She was not in the mood for reason that went against what she knew.

'Who is your pathologist?' he asked her.

'Oh, Simon—will you have a go at him?'

'I'd better have a note from you, authorizing me to talk

to him. It'll probably cost a hundred guineas for him to repeat what he told you.'

'All the same—' Jackie Tasker said.

'All the same—' Kenworthy agreed.

CHAPTER 11

Bishop's Fold is a village within the eastern border of Lancashire and clings to a crest of Pennine fall-line where the backbone of England curves down to the coastal plain. It has a grey, square-towered church, mostly nineteenth-century restored, and two Nonconformist chapels. It also has two grey stone inns and several dozen grey stone cottages which support each other according as they were built—which was without preconception of symmetry, ease of access or social precedence.

Bishop's Fold is a village almost completely without controversy. Such differences of opinion as there are are resolved by compromise—or, more often, by inaction. The only serious subject crops up annually, when the Women's Institute discusses its midsummer outing. The outcome of every deliberation for the last thirty years has been to go to Southport. There is unanswerable precedent for rejecting alternatives: once, just after the war, the Institute travelled to Scarborough, where it rained all day.

This year it was fine again in Southport. The Institute ladies lunched together in their usual restaurant. They walked in their sub-culture groups of two and three up and down the Promenade, and then these lesser units took tea in one or other of the Lord Street cafés. They remembered the waitresses and expected the waitresses to remember them—which most of them did, a tribute to their powers of total recall, for it would be difficult to picture a more average, less distinctive, less memorable cohort than the thirty or so associated matrons of Bishop's Fold, with their chained spectacles, their unadventurous dress-sense, and their monthly competitions for happiest memories, favourite family photographs and most useless kitchen gadgets.

They always left Southport early in the summer evening, always stopped at the Apple Tree at Meyrick-in-Fylde for a dinner of reconstituted minestrone, pellet-fed chicken and lemon meringue pie. And then they set their dusk-drawn headlamps towards the Pennine fall-line, singing 'She'll be coming round the mountain' and 'Roll me over in the clover and do it again'. After that, Minnie Halliday always pretended to resist an invitation to sing 'The Gypsy's Warning', but always surrendered in the end, singing in her seat, with her eyes straight ahead of her; admittedly with a certain untrained ballad sweetness.

When the applause had died down, it was always the cue for the Secretary, little Ann Teagle, to go round with the hat to collect a gratuity for the driver, Len Bingham, whose cropped hair, red neck and yellow cotton coat collar, seen through the glass at the back of his cab, had been a source of confidence to these home-bound women for so many years. (It was an ancient coach, bought by the local garage from North Western when North Western had finished with it, so the driver sat alone in a cubicle. He did not operate from within the main body of the vehicle, as is the usual contemporary practice.)

Before leaving Meyrick-in-Fylde, Len Bingham had drawn the blinds behind him to shield his vision from lights in his rear, so any irregularity in the driving-seat was not apparent to any passenger. Nor—such was the intensity of conversation—did anyone become aware of any aberration in their route until this was well advanced.

Certainly Mrs Doris Somers had said to Mrs Linda Spencer, 'We don't seem to have turned at the Penwortham crossroads yet. Perhaps he's taking us round by Chorley for some reason.' But neither had thought more of it.

Then Elizabeth Turnbull said to Elizabeth Panter, 'I can't think where he's taking us. Surely we're on a motorway—'

They were; and Len Bingham—or somebody—was driving to the upper speed limit. The whisper took notion and shape that Len was taking them home by the M62—and someone was inspired to the theory that this was because of some roadworks that had held them up this morning. This allayed anxiety for a little while, then someone, wiping mist from the glass, saw from a roadsign that they were already south of Warrington.

Now there was a fidget of activity. Messages were passed, and one or two committee members of the breed born for leadership began to squeeze up and down the aisle. The President went and banged on the pane behind Len Bingham's back. When the President of an Institute bangs on a pane behind a man's back, this may usually be counted an imperative gesture. The only response now was pressure on the accelerator.

'Oh dear, what if we're being hi-jacked,' Mrs Panter said to Mrs Turnbull, and the pair of them went into a fit of giggling which, the party knew from experience, was likely to last until their destination. But other councils of war were more practical, and after another hour of careering southwards, Madam President moved back from seat to seat, briefing her members.

But it was not easy to find the ideal moment at which to put her plan into action, and it was not until they had slid into an egress lane and started to trundle through the darkened ways of Staffordshire that the signal was given.

They came into a small market town—they were undecided where—and in its very centre, held up by lights in a traffic-less street, all the windows of the coach were wound down at once. Thirty heads stretched out and the

Bishop's Fold Institute shouted for help.

There was a group of idlers who had clung to a street corner since closing time, and they raised a mighty cheer, mistaking the commotion for middle-aged female coquetry. One man even came over and offered Margery Peacock a mouthful from a can he was holding.

'Don't be daft, man,' she said in her flat East Lancashire vernacular. 'We're being kidnapped.'

At which moment Len Bingham's substitute did a racing start, with his right foot tilting over from the brake to the accelerator pedal, and drove them through the red. It was in this moment that Ann Teagle, fighting the door-handle, made the definitive discovery that they had been locked in.

This was the last reported encounter with the Bishop's Fold coachload. The vehicle was found the next morning ditched on a minor road in the hinterland of Kirkby Stephen, to which it had presumably been driven furiously and empty. Len Bingham also returned to circulation the next day, having been found bound and sticking-plastered in a woodshed behind the Apple Tree at Meyrick-in-Fylde. Concussion confused his evidence, but he remembered getting into his cab, lowering his blind. Then someone had opened his door and something had hit him.

But the substitute for Len Bingham had made one bad mistake. He had overlooked the fact that the coach was fitted with a tachometer—a *spy in the cab*.

'This,' Kenworthy said, 'is not going to be funny. This is what we've known had to come: the real thing. Bedfordshire was a joke. Norfolk held a hint of the sinister. This time they'll ask the full price; and somebody may have to pay it.'

'You still stick to your theory, do you, Simon, that the Manager's had to persuade some client that he can put on a big job worth paying for?'

This was Bransby-Lowndes, leaning back again, still blinding himself with his cigarette smoke.

'Nothing else makes any kind of sense. For my money, it will be a springing from gaol, maybe a multiple one. And if the people at the top waste time, it won't be earrings and ears that will come home to roost. It will be Women's Institute members, one every day or two, expendable and expended.'

'Nasty,' Bransby-Lowndes said. 'With half the press crying out that a halt must be called. And if the Home Secretary decides that there has to be sacrificial mutton—'

'There'll be civil war in Lancashire.'

'No!' Bransby-Lowndes said, with an emphasis that made Kenworthy look at him in a fresh way.

'No. Because you and Forrester are now going to pull the stops out.'

The same day, a memorandum arrived on Hewitson's desk, carbon copy to the Faculty. Two days previously, a body had been turned out of a ditch in marshland Cambridgeshire, disturbed by a machine that was grubbing out centuries-old hedgerows. It was an obscene experience for everyone concerned—and the press spared the public the more convincing detail. (One labourer had thought from the smell that they were into a dead deer.) The body had been there for weeks rather than days—and had been dead longer than that. There was certain evidence—dental work, and a history of orthopædic surgery—that had been circulated to pathologists by Hewitson as part of his extraordinarily comprehensive staffwork. The remains were identified as those of Albert Saxby, sometime Pastor of the Gospel Hall at Morley Mortain.

Forensic went to work on every particle that Albert Saxby had taken with him to his death. Everything that was amenable to microscope or reagent was examined. Stitches in the seams of his clothing were unpicked. The welts of his shoes were combed, dirt was removed from under his fingernails. It was one of the most furiously scavenging exercises ever mounted. Everyone, down to the last test-tube washing steward, seemed to be willing success to the project.

The contents of Albert Saxby's alimentary tract were not officially stated to have been repulsive, even to the experts—but that had been inescapably the case. He had eaten—or, rather bolted—a quantity of chips, not long before digestion had ceased. There was also Cheddar cheese, including a piece of its badly masticated crust. Death had been by a single 9 mm bullet, fired into the spinal cord at the neck from a range of mere inches.

His clothes were informative. There was Cambridgeshire mud in liberal quantity. He seemed to have been dragged through it without respect—as if by one man, who had not been physically up to the task. Deeper in the texture of his trouser-bottoms, there was chalky dust. There was also retrieved from his shoes and the mesh of his socks a pollen identified as the product of *Picris hieraciodes jonsonis*, a fairly rare variety of ox-tongue that is in flower on chalky downs at precisely that month and part of the month when Saxby was last seen by his fellow-travellers.

Millicent Mayhew had stabbed at Wiltshire in her original statement, basing her guess on white stones in the fields—though she had added that that could have been the effect of sunlight.

Hewitson had therefore centred on Wiltshire one of his early surveys of likely country villas. But, as he said to Kenworthy, an exhaustive box-search had been beyond his resources. He was overwhelmed by so many other possibilities that he had had to move on to other things. But now he turned his attention to Wiltshire again. It was what some philosophers called the categorical imperative:

you bring something off when you have to.

In the meanwhile, Kenworthy had had an interview with another pathologist, Dr R. Martin Hunter, the one retained by Jacqueline Tasker. Kenworthy had read his report through forwards and backwards, had done some Reference Library reading, and had questioned Dr Hunter – whom he found, at ten pounds a minute, patient, polite, civilized and pragmatic.

'So what you are telling me, Doctor – and thank you for being so frank – is that in your private belief there is evidence to support the theory that Tasker could have been forcibly hanged?'

Dr Hunter inclined his head.

'That is a subjective conclusion. The subjective is not supposed to enter into it. I fear it often does.'

'And you would not be prepared to maintain the proposition under oath?'

'I would be prepared to suggest it as a possibility. Cross-examination would be sure to impugn it. The final judgement would have to be inconclusive. It would be professional idiocy not to remain open-minded.'

'Thank you, Doctor.'

Kenworthy's next call was at Cranston Green, where he half hoped that a detailed log would be kept of all movements on and off the landings of the punishment block.

'Good God – if we had to do that, we'd spend three-quarters of our time writing. What do we want with that sort of record?'

'We could do with it now,' Kenworthy said.

Major movements in and out of the wing were noted, that was all. Kenworthy called for the residents' list on the day of Tasker's death. He learned nothing helpful from it. He asked to talk to other prisoners who had been on that corridor that day. Of these, four had been discharged and ten transferred. Three were brought to him. He trod carefully. If they spotted that there was something that he'd like them to say, they'd say it for the sake of a single cigarette. He could not unearth a spontaneous hint of any scuffle, screaming or falling about. He noticed the way one of them was catching the Chief Officer's eye. There had been unsavoury insinuations about this gaol before. Some of these men had years to do yet. They knew that it could not pay to let the staff down. Kenworthy found his suspicions about Cranston Green deepening with every minute that he spent in the place. Cynics spoke of cot-deaths. There had been allegations of brutality that had been thrown out in court. There had been one major escape about which enquiry had proved fruitless: it had to have been done with internal connivance.

Kenworthy asked to see the officers who were on duty on the day of Franky's death. Past rosters were dug out: Evans and Leigh. They couldn't be expected to remember as far back as that. It had been no sort of memorable day—except for Franky. And these two had gone off duty by the time the body was found.

Then Evans—who was at least putting on an appearance of trying; Leigh wasn't—did remember something.

'Funny—it hasn't come into my mind from that day to this. There was someone came up. The dentist.'

'Dentist?'

'Yes—he wanted to see Maybury. He had a dental plate for him that had been in for repair.'

'Is it usual for a dentist to come and see a prisoner in his cell? Why not have him down to the surgery?'

'It was only a question of handing the thing over, popping it into his mouth, seeing if it fitted. It saved an escort duty, and there's always a backlog queue for surgery time.'

'You mean this often happens?'

'It's known to.'

'How long was the dentist with Maybury?'

'I can't remember that. A minute or two, I suppose. I wasn't in view all the time. I was called away.'

'Could this dentist have had access to Tasker's cell?'

'He'd have to have had a key.'

'And had he a key?'

'Not supposed to. I had to let him in to see Maybury. And my mate had to let him out again when he hammered the door.'

'But he could have had a key?'

'It would be irregular. Look, sir—the dentist is a prison official. I don't go round suspecting—'

Kenworthy turned to the Chief Officer.

'I think I'd better have a word with Maybury.'

But Maybury did not help. Maybury was not bright. Like others in Cranston Green, he would have told any lie that came to his lips, if he thought he could turn it to his trivial advantage. But he had not the brains to think of the right lies, so his first round had to be to remember nothing at all.

Dentist? Dental plate? He hadn't even got a dental plate. He'd always looked after his teeth. He showed them to Kenworthy. That was why he'd been surprised when a dentist had come up one afternoon. Yes—it was the day poor old Franky Tasker topped himself. Information came out of Maybury strictly an item at a time. Every sliver of it had to be chiselled for. No; he'd told this chopper merchant there must be some mistake. Some clerk must have looked down the names with a squint. Maybury had shown the dentist his teeth. All his own. Had always looked after them. So the dentist had shoved off to find out whose choppers they were.

Hewitson's timetable was in shreds. It was impossible to be where he had to be, to look at everything himself. But he did go to Salisbury Plain. He was convinced by now—and no one knew better than he the danger of such conclusions—that he would find what he was looking for in Wiltshire.

He had driven round the edges of Salisbury, Stonehenge and the army complexes. He cursed himself for spending an aimless day when there was so much else undone. He had a beer and a pie in a pub and walked to the edge of a village. He saw white stones scattered about the tilth of field after field. Millicent Mayhew had been right first go: he knew it. And how far was it going to get him? He stood and looked out at a rolling hill. He needed a stroke of luck. A policeman ought not to invoke luck. He ought not to think in such terms. But in how many big cases—eminent coppers' big cases—had it been luck, just one stroke, that had cracked things finally open?

Then he had his luck. He saw a helicopter. And he knew then how he had to quarter Wiltshire. It took him three hours to locate another helicopter that he could get authority to use, to transmute that authority into a pilot at the controls at an RAF station in Gloucestershire.

They scanned towns, villages and countryside in systematic strips. Hewitson had the feeling that always came to him in Wessex, an awe-inspiring atmosphere of prehistoric tracks and tumuli, of white horses and long men.

And then, on the winding back road between Salisbury and Amesbury, he saw a private road that led to a large house: a house built round an inner court; the court laid out in rose-beds; the line of outer wall broken by bushes and trees, so that from the ground at any distance one was not likely to guess at the layout within.

Excitement—of which the pilot was more demonstrative than Hewitson. The village was Purshill. The villa was shown on the one-inch map as Fosse House. There was nothing behind it but a swell of downs. So back to Gloucestershire, back into his own car, back to Wiltshire for a ground reconnaissance.

*

The long-suffering old coach from Bishop's Fold had put main roads behind itself, had turned into a lane whose twigs and brambles scraped tooth-jarringly across its windows. The surface was unmetalled and it felt as if the suspension would jack it in any minute. Moreover, they started to climb a gradient so steep that even in bottom gear the engine was threatening to stall. They turned into a hairpin bend that was almost too tight for the steering lock.

The President had been a headmistress in her prime, and a first eleven hockey forward in her Training College years. She had the sort of voice, when *ex cathedra* demanded it, that could rally a dispirited team.

'Members of the Bishop's Fold Institute, I believe that we are about to add to our experience. Let us not lose our self-command.'

'Let's hope we lose nothing else,' was the audible comment of one of the more vulgar members of the sorority on the back seat.

'As we arrive wherever we are being taken, I propose to lead you in the singing of "Jerusalem".'

And, as the coach pulled painfully over uneven terrain, the Bishop's Fold Institute, with contributions from voices of varying talent, raised to the heavens their anthem of hope, dedication and battle.

The dentist was Robert Harrington Bryce. He was not a full-time member of the prison service, but a supernumerary, a non-partner in a practice on the edge of Coventry, who was engaged to come in one day a week to help with the overload. There was nothing in the records of the prison dental surgery to suggest how a mistake could possibly have been made over dentures for Maybury.

Kenworthy visited the Coventry practice—but Robert Harrington Bryce was not there. He had developed a streptococcal throat during the course of that morning and had pleaded to retire home to whisky and aspirin. There was no point in his staying to infect patients.

His home was a bachelor apartment. Had he received any phone calls during the course of the morning? The senior partner did not know. The receptionist confirmed that he had. There was nothing exceptional in that.

Robert Bryce was not at his apartment. Kenworthy did not expect him to be. As long as he was in possession of a British passport, he was within his legal rights to be out of the country by now. If he wished to avoid an embarrassing interview, he could be well on his way by now.

No doubt the Manager would be financing his journey.

Hewitson was accompanied by a plainclothes woman sergeant of the Wiltshire CID. He was posing as a door-to-door market researcher, she as his trainee. They practised their arts at a number of doors before aiming them direct at Fosse House. This enabled Hewitson to elicit the information that the house belonged to an anchorite of a scientist, believed by some to be mad and by very many to be an ardent vivisectionist. But he had been away from home longer than a year, and it was known that the house had been let furnished. But to whom? The nearest other home was half a mile away; but even here they had no information about the unknown lessees.

From the Manager's point of view, Fosse House had to be remote; remote it was. It was hidden by tall pines from being overlooked by any other habitation. Hewitson and his assistant—whom he found thoroughly charming—found no sign of human presence. Shutters were firmly secured from within as well as without. The gardens gave the impression of being well tended as a rule, but of not having been touched for a fortnight or so: lawns growing welt-deep, incipient bindweed exploring the borders, fallen petals unswept.

Breaking and entering would have to be savage and noisy and was beyond Hewitson's ability without equipment and a team. He foresaw very great difficulty over getting a warrant with such evidence as he would be able to present.

'Till we have built Jerusalem,
In England's green and pleasant land.'

The Bishop's Fold WI was kept waiting in its seats for a long time before the coach door was opened. Those by the windows on the right-hand side could see a coming and going of torchlights, then the switching on of a lamp above a door which showed them to be in a large, untidy—and in fact disused—farmyard. The buildings were of rough-hewn limestone, and those who had paid the shrewdest attention to their route diagnosed one of the wilder tracts of Derbyshire.

They sang 'Jerusalem' a second time, but the third repetition began to waver. Madam President used the rallying tone with which she might have encouraged a short corner, and this inspired renewed effort in about two-thirds of her flock.

Those who had been near enough to see the driver jump down from his cab were now finally assured that this was not Len Bingham, but a fatter, more beery, surly-looking man, with thicker hair than Len's and his eyes wider apart. Now that a few of the women caught sight of him face-on, there seemed something somehow obscene about the substitution.

The singing finally died entirely away and a nervous silence gripped the coach. Gossip had lost all piquancy. No one wanted to talk. The only certainty was that the coach's heater was now no longer working.

Then a man crossed the yard with a key in his hand, ready to insert it in the lock. He was a small man, fleshless and weathered, and he had in both frame and features that appearance of static age that some men carry from their forties to the onset of their seventies. He came aboard and inhaled ready to address the travellers, which he did in dry London vowels, of which these north-countrywomen were very conscious. He spoke in tones and terms that army warrant officers have been known to use when introducing themselves to freshly arrived recruits.

'My name is Webbe. I am in charge of your security and comfort until such time as, we hope, we shall set you on the road for home again. There will be some of you who will be wondering what you are in for, and a few who may wish that at this very moment you were tucked up in your own beds at home.'

He paused for smiles at least, but did not actually look for long at any of the eyes that were focused on him.

'Well: there is nothing that you or I can do about that. You are here until certain clear and simple requirements have been carried out, and I am here to see to your every-day necessities. All you have to do is to carry out without fuss or argument such instructions as you may from time to time be given. There is nothing for any of you to worry about, because your thinking is going to be done for you. Give us no trouble, and there is no need for any of you to get hurt or be uncomfortable. You play fair with me, and I'll play fair with you. Now I want you to stand up, two at a time, beginning at the front on my left-hand side, get off the bus and follow the directions you'll be given.'

But Madam President was by no means as amenable as Sergeant-Major Webbe seemed to hope. She got up from her seat and advanced on him.

'If you think that we are simply going to accept this—'

'Now, my dear lady—anything you wish to say to me had better be saved until we get indoors.'

He extended his arms, put his hands on her shoulders,

and attempted to push her back into her seat.

'Take your hands off our President!'

That was the Secretary, wilful Ann Teagle, smaller than Webbe himself, but *ex officio* an uncompromising defender of the constitution and dignity of Institute procedure. She too left her seat and, swinging her handbag through almost three hundred and sixty degrees, caught the Sergeant-Major unambiguously across the side of his face with it.

CHAPTER 12

The search of Fosse House was carried out with full regard for everything that had to be regarded: the warrant and a large team of local officers, strictly enjoined on the incompatible themes of thoroughness and damage.

There was junk mail on the mat, in the hall an oil-painting of a stormy sea, such as Farmer Ketteringham had reported. And upstairs there was plenty of evidence that this was the place in which both Morley Mortain and Binney St Botolph had been detained: single bedrooms and a house-telephone in each room, the lines dead. There was a harsh austerity in the prisoners' furnishings: divan beds and a single chair each. But in box-rooms above was a store of television sets, of bedside carpets, stereograms, writing-tables and a variety of prints and hangings. It really took only a few little touches, some of them relatively inexpensive, to switch from bareness to an impression of *luxe*.

Elsewhere were staff quarters, efficiently stripped of anything that might leave a clue to personality. Whoever had done the security inspection after the departure of the main body, had known what he was about. The same was true of a downstairs suite that had clearly been used as an operations room. Millicent Mayhew had spoken of their being able to communicate with a receptionist. The switchboard was plain to see: but it bore no traces of the character and tastes of its operator. It was going to have to be a case, yet again, of *minutiæ*—of dust from corners, and scrapings from the inside walls of dustbins. There would be the question of who paid the rates, the electricity, the phone bills: but by now Hewitson knew the Manager well enough to know that all those things would have been covered by a faceless and untraceable agency. The Manager thought of all things in advance—

He wanted to stay and see the Fosse House search through to an advanced stage, but there were too many tangential tasks crowding in on him. For the first time in his career, Hughie Hewitson was doubting his ability to cope with his plateful. He hurried back to London.

And at New Scotland Yard, well after what most men would consider office hours, a Commander and an Assistant Commissioner were waiting to take him into conference.

'What's kept you in Wiltshire so long?'

They already knew from the telex about the abandoned headquarters.

'I thought this was it,' Hewitson said.

'You've got to learn, Hewitson, that the General Officer Commanding an army does not go out and lead forward patrols, even if he thinks he can do it better than a line-unit subaltern. Your job is to command and co-ordinate.'

'We keep finding new trails, sir. We keep narrowing gaps. We never seem to close one.'

'And while you're out trying to do other men's work for them, news of new gaps keeps dropping on your desk. Now there's a fresh line of enquiry for you to follow up,' the Assistant Commissioner said. 'Put an inspector and three on it. Start looking for the man who reconnoitred Morley,

Binney and Bishop's Fold.'

It had been a thought so far removed from immediate action that Hewitson had put it off for secondary attention.

'We've tended to think of Morley Mortain as a random pick-up. A security van cruises through Bedfordshire, finds a shop full of people, loads them aboard. I no longer think that was done at random. Somebody knew for certain that between nine and half past on a Monday morning was Dolly Mason's busiest half-hour. Somebody had been and seen. When that Norfolk parish council met, somebody knew about it in advance. Somebody had been and asked. And somebody must have known, not only that the Women's Institute was going to Southport, but also where they would stop for their evening meal. They must have known what sort of coach they were going in, because it had to be the kind with the driver isolated in his cab—'

So Hewitson started combing his resources to see what spare inspector-time he could find—on paper, an unpromising topic. He encroached ruthlessly on overtime and rest-days: there were one or two other channels that he wanted to initiate before the AC and the Commander had him in again.

So it was a new face that called at Millicent Mayhew's craft shop: an Inspector Gibson, who rather looked as if he had been in last year's sixth form. It was a pity that he should be the fourth stranger to try to refresh her memory. Miss Mayhew was amicable to all callers, but did not become forthcoming until acquaintanceship developed. Barrington Watts of the *Examiner* had laboured hard in the initial stages. Even Kenworthy had made only the faintest dents in her determination not to besmirch her neighbours' reputations. Gibson, wondering after his first mouthful how he was going to dispose of the contents of his coffee-cup, was compelled to sit back and listen to an entire side of Hindemith's *Four Temperaments*. Only then could he edge in the critical question.

'Miss Mayhew, it is essential that we learn everything we can about the liaisons that Pastor Saxby made while you were detainees.'

'But I have already explained, to Mr Kenworthy and to others, that I see no point in befouling by hearsay—'

'Miss Mayhew, Pastor Saxby has been found dead.'

'Then *de mortuis nil nisi*—'

'I respect that, Miss Mayhew. I may say that Mr Hewitson and Mr Kenworthy greatly admire you for it. But the question is: how many more have got to die?'

'I can hardly think that Pastor Saxby died because he made the belated discovery of his own biochemistry, Mr Gibson.'

Gibson looked at her covertly. There was a discreet note on the file that it looked as if she had made a first discovery of some of her own undreamed-of potential whilst under confinement in Fosse House.

'You seem pretty certain that he did make such a discovery,' Gibson said.

'You won't catch me out like that, young man.'

She was a difficult woman to influence by oblique threats. Even to be taken and held for twelve or twenty-four hours in the nearest headquarters might be a new experience in which she would find interest. You couldn't even appeal to her citizenship, because she was the sort of woman who paid greater attention to her obligations in a larger cosmos.

'His death could have been a crime of simple jealousy,' he said.

'I don't think so.'

'You have reasons for saying that?'

Millicent Mayhew could not help smiling at some sweetly private memory.

'He simply took advantage of what was, to quote the phrase beloved of our village shop, on offer.'

'On offer by Rita Lonsdale?'

'Mr Gibson, I cannot say. Whatever happened between Albert Saxby and Rita Lonsdale was not performed as a public spectacle.'

'I suppose not. But it would be a talking point among the rest of your party.'

'Mr Kenworthy drew a parallel with Somerset Maugham's story *Rain*. The pastor was obviously under compulsion to attend to Rita Lonsdale's salvation. The general opinion was that she had ideas of her own about his: and managed to appeal to something inexperienced in him. But you are not suggesting that he was murdered for the sake of Rita Lonsdale?'

'By no means. But I think you could tell us for whose sake he might have been murdered.'

'Then my supposition could become your working suspicion.'

'I am merely suggesting that certain of his appetites were whetted – and that there were certain other services *on offer*. Pastor Saxby may have gone on to save other mortal souls.'

Miss Mayhew gave a little laugh.

'Mr Gibson, you look too young to know about such things.'

'I think you are being unhelpful, Miss Mayhew. And once that word is noted on your file, I fear you might come in for a good deal of disagreeable attention.'

'That would be annoying. But whom am I supposed to help? I simply do not want to say anything that I do not know for certain to be true.'

'Even if you could prevent charges from being made against the wrong person?'

That is what did it. He could see that the thought brought her up short, and she conned it over for a few seconds.

'All right – against my better judgement, I will tell you. You have been very clever. There was a young lady among those who waited on us. She said her name was Saroyah. I think she was half Persian. A most attractive child. Supple. Always smiling. She spent a good deal of time with Albert Saxby, and he with her.'

It could hardly be bilateral and unilateral at the same time, could it? But Gibson saw the dangers in a verbal quibble at this stage. He said nothing.

'It was after we had been there about a week—and there had obviously been some quite serious tiff between him and Rita. I think perhaps that after things had gone a certain way between them, he tried to return to undiluted evangelism. The next thing we observed were signs that the pastor and Saroyah seemed to be taking things very seriously indeed.'

'In fact, Saroyah was carrying out the role for which she was on the strength of Fosse House?'

'If that is so, she was a very good actress. I am an old maid with very limited experience of such things; but perhaps that makes me an objective observer. I would have said that Saroyah was genuinely in love with Albert.'

Gibson also called on Farmer Ketteringham. Ketteringham was not disposed to give time, thought or imagination to his problems.

'I tell you, I know nothing more than I have said and signed. As far as I'm concerned, the affair is over. I've lost enough working time this season—'

'Mr Ketteringham, there are points that have cropped up, and—'

'Then you'd better go off and find someone else who can answer them. I was made to eat porridge made of meal that I wouldn't—'

'All I want to know, Mr Ketteringham, is whether there were any strangers in the village making enquiries about the next meeting of the parish council.'

'I don't know why anyone should want to do that.

There's no interest shown in the council by the village, let alone strangers. And now, if you'll excuse me, I've got to get on the phone to have a beast castrated.'

He appeared to think it would be no bad idea to have Gibson dealt with on the same domiciliary visit.

'You heard of no one in the pub, asking questions about local politics? Nobody giving out to be a reporter, for example?'

'Hold you hard. Now that there was. That would be a week or two before we were took. Young man, he was. Wanted to know about the coypu. That's got to be a pest here, in the ditches. Gets in the beet-piles. Eats its own weight in a day or two. He wanted to know if the Parish Council planned any action.'

'And does it?'

'I told him to go off and see Min. Ag. Parish rate don't run to a wave of vermin.'

'I see. Did he show any other interest in your Parish Council?'

'Well, he wanted to know what sort of thing we did do, if we couldn't attend to pests. And then -- yes, that's it -- '

A fresh memory did not exactly excite Joe Ketteringham, but it stirred up another sentence.

'He wanted to know was the public admitted to council meetings, and when was the next one going to be.'

'Can you give me a description of this man? Had he a car?'

Ketteringham was not a born portrayer of his fellows. He would have said that this stranger had two eyes, for the simple reason that he would have expected him to have had. The inspector had taken thousands of descriptions in his time, and knew how to ask fruitful questions. But for all that, he came away with notes that could have applied to several million: aged in his later thirties, no hat, abundant curly hair, height about 5 ft 9 ins, casual grey-blue check suit. And an R registration yellow Escort.

At last something positive to send to Hewitson.

From Morley Mortain confirmation came of another piece of Millicent Mayhew's evidence. In a neighbouring village the brick kilns had been idle for some months because of recession in the building trade. Now a demand had come in that made inroads into stockpiles for a programme of inner city development. A skeleton work-force was set on and it was discovered that one of the stacks of bricks had been interfered with in a purposeful way. Bricks had been taken away from the middle so as to turn the stack into a hollow square, its roof a single course of bricks laid over timbers. There were the tracks of a medium-heavy vehicle inside this improvised garage.

Was this the tunnel in which the Morley Mortain party had changed from one van to another? Was this unskilled building operation one that could have been carried out without exciting public attention? Answer: obviously—it had been. Two or three men, working quietly and with system, could achieve it in a couple of hours of darkness.

The track marks were cast in plaster for the experts.

The couple who had been set on the tachometer recording from the Bishop's Fold bus ran into one frustration after another. Since the graph from the *spy in the cab* showed a plotting of time against speeds, it should have been possible in theory to trace the bus absolutely to its destination, especially since a stop was recorded at the very time when a group of merry males had indulged in cross-purpose banter at traffic lights in a small town. The next morning, when the loss of the Institute had been made known, two of the males had been public-spirited enough to report the incident to their friendly neighbourhood constable, and it was possible to pinpoint the place as Hammerford, half way between Uttoxeter and Ashbourne.

This information was treated with premature jubilation.

It surely broke the back of the journey for the detectives. But when they tried to apply the record to the map, they ran into all kinds of difficulty. Within the twenty miles beyond Hammerford, there were many combinations of crossroads and roundabouts which the driver must surely have taken recklessly, for his dips of deceleration did not seem to bear any relationship to the vagaries of the roads. Moreover, he seemed to have used a diversionary tactic some two miles short of his destination, which involved several U-turns followed by short stretches in reverse: either because he was trying to confuse his passengers (as had happened to the Bedfordshire party) or because he had overshot a turning and was trying to do a three-point turn in a lane too narrow for the manœuvre.

The couple tried to reconstruct the journey in reverse from the long stretch from the destination to Kirkby Stephen, where the coach had been finally abandoned. But here they struck even more confusing snags. The record of speeds was such that the driver must have followed a route that no man in his senses would have chosen: and, indeed, must surely have exceeded the necessary distance. It had been thought at first that he had made a bad mistake by leaving the tachometer intact and functioning. Now it began to look as if this had been done deliberately, with intent to mislead. An odd feature was that some two miles after setting out back for the north, the coach had once again done this peculiar sequence of stop, start and reverse. So who was the driver trying to fool that time?

The two officers gave up their attempts to solve the problem on the table, and tried driving the course, following in turn a dozen combinations of routes after Hammerford, the man in the passenger-seat calling out speeds and distances. It was hopeless. Temporary traffic-lights at roadworks threw out their calculations, and the pilot made so many errors of mental arithmetic that he became incapable of clear thought. There were long stretches when the Institute's bus had well exceeded the legal limits, and it was impossible to maintain such speeds by daylight. At other stages, incomprehensible sloth had lorries hooting and snorting behind them. The pair submitted a report arguing the futility of the calculation, and were returned to the case-load from which they had been seconded.

Now Hewitson borrowed an inspector and a sergeant from Met Traffic and told them to tackle the problem afresh from scratch. By this time, Hewitson's reputation for pleasantness in personal relationships was beginning to wear thin.

'For God's sake, do it by night. And before you set out, get a note from Staffs and all adjoining counties of what roadworks and temporary obstructions their highways departments had in hand on the night in question.'

Herbert Spriggs—wearing, as he always did, for public appearances, a London bus conductor's hat with a red band round it—was exercising that originality of wit which still brought a smile of enjoyment to the eyes of his attentive listeners.

'Seven and six, was she worth it?—Legs, eleven—'

At the end of the session, when the winners and the losers had departed, and he was doing a favour for old Adam Greenwood by locking up the Village Hall, Herbert Spriggs, the Morley Mortain Bull, was aware of a shadowy female figure waiting to waylay him under cover of the porch: old Aggie Lonsdale. And that was sufficient reminder of a previous encounter to set his digestion on the wrong track.

'Listen, Herbert—you know my Rita's got another in the oven?'

'Well, it isn't me this time. Not that I've ever been too damned sure it was last time, though I do let her have five nicker a week when I'm not on the Club.'

'Yes—you're on it, and she's in it. But hold your horses, nobody's blaming you. You had enough to keep you busy with Mrs Broad, according to what my Rita says. She reckons it's Albert Saxby that's tipped the man out the boat this time.'

'Well, she'll not get much more out of Albert Saxby from where he's gone.'

'That's the whole point, Herbert. I reckon she's got a claim against his estate.'

'Estate? What estate has Saxby left? Stack of hymn-books and a harmonium on the blink.'

'The man must have had something to his name. And he'd no one else to leave it to, had he? What I was thinking is, if you were to give evidence—'

'What bloody evidence can I give? I wasn't actually in bed with them.'

'No. But you knew what was going on.'

'It didn't go on for long,' Spriggs said.

'It doesn't take all that bloody long, either, does it? Rita says he only had to come near her.'

'I don't mean that. He didn't stick all that long with Rita. A foreign piece—well, half foreign—'

'Rita said she wasn't. Said she was as English as Max Bygraves. And I want you down at the solicitor's with me and Rita tomorrow morning, else Rita swears she'll clobber you with this one, too.'

Walter Ulliatt and Samuel Scales were quietly, unostentatiously friends in Grendon Underwood: not to the exclusion of other inmates, and not creating an impression of conspiracy, except perhaps in the eyes of an observer who had been forewarned to expect just that. They did not necessarily sit together to eat, they did not seek each other out at any particular time of day. But it was easy to see that they did come together—alone together—for a certain period every day: sometimes in a corner of a common room, sometimes in a corner of the grounds. If one came close enough to hear what they were talking about, it was football, or their offsprings' post-university inclinations—or the idiosyncrasies of new inmates—for even an Open prison is a restricted society where such things loom large. Their relationship was in fact casual and indifferent—not at all unlike the relationship between Detective-Sergeant Edward Jarman and Detective-Constable Norman Jones, who were the two men planted in Grendon Underwood to watch for the effect of the arrival of William Waterlow.

Walter Ulliatt's sphere was used cars: vast parking lots occupied by them, at nodal points of strategical importance that might possibly have been leased to him through the good services of the entrepreneurial Waterlow. Ninety per cent of Ulliatt's business had always been legitimate, adulterated only by such practices as are not uncommon in his particular trade. Eighty-five per cent of stolen cars are returned to their owners within seventy-two hours; the minority business which had brought Ulliatt to Grendon Underwood had to do with what happened to some of the other fifteen per cent. These were prestige cars, not family runabouts, and Ulliatt had become an expert in export procedures, the replacement of missing or inconvenient documentation, and such technicalities as the counterfeiting of new engine and chassis numbers.

Samuel Scales was in insurance, allied to the investment trusts of private pension schemes: not the pension schemes of large concerns, and not insurance companies of national renown—though some of his little ones had had short periods of unexpected prosperity. It helped small insurance companies when substantial pension funds were invested in them. William Waterlow, too, had come unstuck over insurance, when he had tried to bribe a Company Secretary to be underwritten by a lesser firm, and a larger firm had decided to put an end to such competition.

DS Jarman and DC Jones had been well briefed. They watched Waterlow arrive at Grendon—but there was little to report. Ulliatt was actually checking out at the office when Waterlow was brought in, but no sign of recognition passed between them. Scales sat next to Waterlow at the supper table, but from the way they introduced themselves to each other, it seemed reasonable to conclude that this was their first meeting.

Nevertheless, before twenty-four hours had passed, the three had been seen walking together in the grounds.

Kenworthy and Elspeth were watching Sir Robin Day tie up a backbench spokesman on law and order when the doorbell rang. This time Jackie Tasker was wearing a velvet band round her forehead, into which she had stuck a large and upright feather. Her main apparel was a simple shift, apparently made from a horse-blanket and her cosmetic basis was a kind of terracotta, such as one might make by dissolving a powdered plantpot in vegetable oil.

'Mohican,' she said, in reply to Kenworthy's politely subdued glance of enquiry.

But there was nothing of the North American Indian about the companion she had brought with her, an uneasy character between youth and middle age who appeared to combine the shifty and the shiftless in fairly equal proportions.

'I don't think you've met Bert Tandy, Mr Kenworthy,' she said.

Kenworthy wondered where the *Mr* had suddenly returned from. He guessed that it would have set Tandy's nerves on edge to have seen her too intimate with the law.

'No. I think he's been kept out of circulation by others than me,' he said agreeably.

'That's just it, Mr Kenworthy. Bert came out last Friday from Cranston Green.'

'I was set up, Mr Kenworthy,' Bert Tandy said.

Jackie Tasker turned on him.

'Mr Kenworthy doesn't want to know about that. He wants to know what you told me in the Duchess of Marlborough last night.'

Bert Tandy moistened his lips as if he were not sure whether he had retained the power of speech.

'As long as he knows that I had nothing to do with any of this,' he said.

'Mr Kenworthy knows everything about the likes of you.'

Tandy looked as if he needed to compose the whole paragraph before he uttered the first syllable.

'It's just that in the chokey block at Cranston, Mr K—well, the duty screws, they run a five-card brag school in their office. Well, it isn't an office, really, it's an empty peter—that means a cell—on the end of the landing. And they let prisoners out of their cells to make the school up. Day in, day out—and they'll take money from them—take money from blokes that are supposed to be on bread and water. Do you think that's right, Mr Kenworthy? Don't you think men ought to be doing the job they're paid for, not taking the snout money off the cons?'

'Let's hope the cons occasionally win a bit of it back.' Kenworthy said.

'Never mind the indignation, Bert. Tell Mr Kenworthy how they get away with it, day in day out.'

'Well, they're nicely placed, you see. If the Assistant Governor comes on the wing, they hear his feet on the iron stairs while he's still two landings away. So there's time for everybody to be otherwise engaged by the time he's fetched up alongside. That's how a bloke can bust up his cell and nobody takes a blind bit of notice. That's how Nicky Salt got chivved.'

Jackie Tasker was already making moves to get out of her chair.

'And that's how assistant dentists can hang about a lot

longer than they need.'

Elspeth offered coffee.

'No, thank you. Coffee's bad for Bert's nerves. And I'm late already for a pow-wow in Kenwood.'

She drove Bert Tandy out of the Kenworthys' house with almost indecent urgency.

The Manager made known the asking price, and as everyone had forecast, it was a steep one. Unsurprisingly, it was a list of men to be released from custody. There were the three brothers Jack, Gordon and Alfie Topham, whose gang activities in the 1960s had inspired the judge to recommend a minimum of thirty years in two of their cases. There were the two 'brothers' Bunting—actually they were cousins—whose ingenious sadism had enabled them to protect an area bounded by Dean Street, Oxford Street, Leicester Square and the Charing Cross Road. There was an unsubtle operator called Albert Boardman who had on two occasions fractured night watchmen's skulls with iron bars. And there was a miscellany of less distinguished offenders for whose achievements Hewitson had to go to Central Records: men like David Rowbotham, 'Knácker' Wyatt, Billy Carlyon, 'Bomber' Houston—and that Maybury who boasted that he still had his own teeth.

In interested quarters there was inconclusive decision as to what common thread could possibly unite this disparate gallery. It was the common belief that the hostility between the Tophams and the Buntings was such that they would not make common cause, even to secure their own release. Someone suggested however that the Manager's price for this piece of impudence had been so high that there had had to be a combination of improbables to raise the wind. A counter-theory was that the Manager had no interest whatever in the Tophams or the Buntings, and that they had been included on the roll of releases merely as cover for those who really mattered: Rowbotham, Wyatt, Carlyon, Boardman, Houston and Maybury—one, all, or some.

Hewitson therefore found yet another inspector to dig deep into biographies.

Mr Christopher Medlock rose to ask the Home Secretary if he had any statement to make as to his intentions in the matter of Topham, Bunting, Rowbotham *et al.*

THE HOME SECRETARY: This is a matter of deep concern to us all. I am sure that Honourable Members would not wish me to make any public statement at this juncture that could prejudice the round-the-clock efforts that are being made—

A VOICE: Has he tried stopping the clock?

THE HOME SECRETARY: I am sure the whole country will join with me in agreeing that these anarchical demands have been going on too long. This is a crime with which we are mercifully unfamiliar in the United Kingdom. We must take great care to avoid the impression that perpetrators of this crime can rely on getting away with it. The time has come to call a halt.

ANOTHER VOICE: Does he perhaps believe that the time has also come to call a halt to the Bishop's Fold Women's Institute?

CHAPTER 13

Hewitson was not the only one who felt the need to fine down his approach to the complexities. Kenworthy was also aware that he was sliding about on an icy surface with less sense of direction than he remembered in any investigation in his life. In his case—especially since the hours he kept were largely of his own choosing—he had an uncomfortable feeling of not belonging. He had temporarily lost Wright, who had been called back to Fraud for a few days to develop one of his interim reports. Forrester, bouncing as ever with his image of activity, was only partially applying himself to the Manager. There were other concerns on his horizon: confidential career-reports on the short list for Chief Constable in a north-west conurbation; a study of nominees for vacancies on a regional race relations panel. Bransby-Lowndes, inscrutable and cocksure, seemed forever less concerned with the content of reports than with the mode of their presentation to ministers.

There was too much of everything. Kenworthy felt a sudden surge of sympathy for the Churchillian *Pray let me have on one side of a sheet of paper*—He took his ballpoint and his single sheet of paper and did an elimination exercise. He did it more than once, varying his priorities: and every time he was left with a single name, alone on a line—Franky Tasker.

He decided there and then that he would concentrate on Franky. There were too many questions about Franky that had been taken for granted. The mice, for example: a smelly joke—but in the light of Franky's aversion, a hideous personal one. It depended on just how pathological the aversion was: it could come into the category of a very cruel joke indeed. Kenworthy did not believe it, but that busy little cageful might in fact have driven Franky to hang himself. Then there remained the possibility, as Jackie had first believed, that Franky had had to be murdered because Kenworthy had visited him in Cranston Green. But no—that was not exact. Franky had been killed after Shiner's investigator had been clumsy over his enquiry into the Taskers' standard of life. Was that because the Manager, who had his own ways of knowing what was going on, was afraid that Franky was going to blow something? Why *now*? Franky had been inside before. He had been questioned, cajoled, terrorized, offered favours hundreds of times before—but he had never grassed. Why should they fear that he was going to grass now? Answer that, and the key to a number of unknowns might turn sweetly against the tumblers.

Kenworthy went that evening to Branwell House, one of those GLC blocks of the nineteen-thirties, on the fringes of Bethnal Green and Mile End, that had somehow been missed by bombers and V weapons, and that dominated the mesh of railways, canals and barrack-like Board Schools like some monument of a more stubborn age. Kenworthy had been to Branwell House before. In the days when he had been working his way round and up the London divisions, it had been no uncommon thing for a detective in the field to drop in on the hangers-on of someone who had gone quietly. Often it was a way in to other things that were going on. Sometimes a personal relationship developed, though seldom warm, and with both sides excusing their tolerance in heavily comic fashion.

There had certainly never been any warmth—or comedy—between Kenworthy and Lil Tasker. Franky's wife was too self-sufficient for that. Adversity was something from which she never expected to be free; and adversity in her early married years, when Franky was likely to be sent down any week of the month, was a harsh and familiar pinch. The two sides accepted each other. When Kenworthy gave Lil the odd ten shillings, it was because she must surely need it. He was buying nothing from her. And although she thanked him perfunctorily, he knew she hated herself for having to take it.

It was a similar relationship when he called on her now. Wordlessly she turned her shoulders to him for him to follow her into the flat. She was ironing and went straight back to her board, not smiling, not scowling, not even particularly looking at him.

'Cup of tea?'

That was not hospitality; it was something that it was her social duty to provide. In a peculiar way that had hated him for his faults, she had loved Franky. Despite him, she had kept things going for him. Now Franky was dead. He was dead because of Kenworthy. There was no way in which she couldn't be thinking that. She'd know that Kenworthy had retired. Maybe she'd heard along the grapevine that he was sitting in with a watching brief. It did not matter. It was not something that he needed to explain to her. He was Kenworthy. Franky was dead because the world appointed its Kenworthys.

'I'd like a cup,' he said.

She put her iron down with neither speed nor sloth, went over to fill the kettle. He noticed that she did not set a cup and saucer for herself. She was not going to drink with him. That was her way of making a statement about the way things stood between them.

'How often were you visiting Franky?' he asked her.

'Once a month – as per entitlement.'

'When did you last go?'

'Last month.'

'How long before – ?'

'Two weeks.'

'Did you notice anything?'

'What would there be to notice?'

'Did he seem depressed at all? They said at the inquest—'

'He hadn't enough sense to be depressed, Mr Kenworthy. Franky never was a man to look on the black side. He was a man who couldn't see the black side coming. That was more than half the trouble with him: too much confidence.'

The kettle was already boiling. It was brand new, a three-kilowatt element.

'Did he say anything to you about mice?'

'It was before the mice.'

'When did you first get to hear about them?'

'Afterwards. Jackie told me after she'd been to you.'

'Have you any ideas about them?'

'Somebody getting at him. Somebody trying to send him out of his mind.'

'He was as bad as that about the things, was he?'

She did not answer that. Somehow her silence conveyed inexpressible horror.

'When and how did it start, his antipathy to mice?'

The door of the bathroom opened. Kenworthy turned and saw Jackie come out, wigless, her own hair short, brown and spiky, her small head spherical, her face clean of make-up. She was wearing a dressing-gown of pink towelling, tightly belted. He did not think she had anything on under it at all.

'Does it matter?' Lil Tasker asked.

'I think it does.' Jackie had heard the question. Her mother looked at her with distaste.

'Go and get dressed.'

'He got it from his stupid mother, Mr Kenworthy. Some women end up with their kids scared stiff of thunderstorms. With my grandmother, it was mice. She couldn't have been more terrified of scorpions. And she'd plenty to go on, because their house was crawling with them. And when Dad's father died, and the coffin was open in their little front room, he could hear the mice scrambling in and out of it. And he believed that if one of them came upstairs, and under his door and over his bed, he'd catch something off it, and then he'd die too. He was six.'

'A load of old cobblers,' her mother said.

'It's true, Mum. That's how it started. And it lasted all his childhood. Do you know, Mr Kenworthy, he'd even shrink back from the sight of one dead? He couldn't stand the sight of one's tail, sticking out from under a cupboard. I know. I played a silly trick on him once with a piece of elastic band.'

'What does it matter?' Lil Tasker said.

'You must excuse me. I must go and get ready.'

Jackie went into her bedroom. Lil Tasker put pressure on a handkerchief.

'I think it matters,' Kenworthy said. 'How widely known was this phobia of Franky's? Among his associates I mean.'

'He could hardly keep it dark, could he?'

Jackie had left her bedroom door open. She did not mean to miss this conversation.

'He was ashamed of it,' she shouted. 'He didn't want people to get to know, or he'd have jokes played on him.'

'Exaggerated,' her mother said.

'There's no exaggeration, Mum. You know as well as I do, he came unstuck on one job because there was a mouse in a place they'd broken into. Dad and Dave Rowbotham. Dad jumped back and dropped an armful of golfing trophies.'

'That isn't true. Dave was making it up, trying to be funny.'

Jackie had come to her bedroom door in a bra and the briefest of briefs. Her body-skin was very white, her belly flat, her navel neat and smooth.

'Jackie—for God's sake!'

'It'll do Mr Kenworthy no harm to know what I'm like under some of the things he's seen me wearing.'

'Jackie!'

'Dave Rowbotham,' Kenworthy said. 'Now that name's familiar. Didn't I see it in this morning's paper? Isn't he on the latest list—a candidate for premature release? Do you know him well, this Dave Rowbotham? He's not one I ever came across.'

Lil Tasker did not want to discuss him.

'Franky knocked about with him at one time,' she admitted.

'Brought him home now and then, did he?'

'That was something I didn't encourage.'

'Oh, Mum—'

Jackie was leaning round her door again. She had put on a pair of pink baggy trousers, low in the crotch and taped tightly round the ankles—the sort worn by some Muslim women, and those aping their style.

'Oh, Mum—you know you fancied him! I had to call him Uncle Dave, Mr Kenworthy. And sometimes when Dad was away—let's say on business—I'd be given a few bob to go to the flicks with Kath Brightie. If I played my cards right, I might be given a few bob by both parties.'

Lil Tasker crossed the room in fury and closed the bedroom door with a crash. They could hear Jackie laughing.

'Kids! I don't know what we have them for! There isn't a word of truth in that, Mr Kenworthy.'

She was taking the slur very much to heart. There were old-fashioned threads of morality and modesty in Lil Tasker.

'But tell me more about this Rowbotham.'

'I tell you, I hardly knew him. He was bad medicine for Franky. My one thought was to be rid of him. Luckily, he was away as often as Franky was.'

'And always at the same time?'

'They came and went. Not always together.'

'What was his main line?'

'Anything. And his ideas worked less often than Franky's did—which is saying a lot. Franky was small-time, God knows—but he was ha'pennies. Dave Rowbotham was washers. Look, it's no use asking me for information, Mr Kenworthy. I know no more about Dave Rowbotham than I do about Jack the Ripper.'

'It seems funny that his name should be on this release list. Unless he's done some big deal somewhere or other, he hardly seems to be of interest to high level people.'

'High level people? Big deal? Dave Rowbotham? Pinching off market stalls, more likely—and getting caught.'

'What sort of age is the man?'

'Mr Kenworthy, can we talk about something else, please? Something I know something about?'

There was a raw spot here, and it was Jackie who had scratched it open.

'Well, do you know anyone else on the list, then? It strikes me as curious that there should be a little bunch like this, some of whose paths never seem to have crossed—'

'Mr Kenworthy, for God's sake! When Franky was alive, I closed my eyes as much as I could to the company he kept. Now he's gone, I want out of it altogether.'

'Granted. But one of the things I always admired about you was the way you kept Franky out of all the trouble you could. To do that, you had to have a very shrewd idea who was who among his mates.'

'And it's all finished with. I want to forget it.'

'Answer this question, then I promise I'll let you. Is there any man at all on this morning's list who rings a bell—because of connection with Franky?'

'There is not.'

'Now if I were to find such a connection later on, I might wonder why you hadn't wanted to tell me.'

'I'm not a liar, Mr Kenworthy. You were good enough never to harass me while Franky was alive. I don't know why you've started now. I never soiled my fingertips. I never let myself be drawn in. I'm not going to be drawn in now—on either side.'

Perhaps—just perhaps—the lady was protesting too much. In the worst years of her life, Lil Tasker had kept her cool. Why was she losing it now? Hadn't the all-clear sounded? Was this post-grief reaction? Or something more sinister? Someone or other—G. K. Chesterton, was it?—once said that the only way to see a thing properly was to stand on your head to look at it. Kenworthy tried an experiment with Lil Tasker, mentally turned her upside down, examined her from unusual angles.

She was a worn-down East End housewife. She seldom went further than the Seabright Street supermarket. She went to the pub not more than once a week—and then not every week. She had a daughter who was in the money—the Manager's money.

Could Lil have been the brains that linked Franky with the Manager? How close to the Manager might she be? The Manager had to have his regional executives—someone to deal with recruitment, selection, distribution of welfare. Could it have been Lil who had first had Franky introduced into more elite circles than he was accustomed to? Might she have got him, for example, the recurring job of organizing traffic hold-ups in places where there was going to be a police chase—or where it would help to have a squad car pinned down?

Suppose there had been—still was—something between Lil and Uncle Dave Rowbotham? Suppose she were near enough to the Manager to know that a list was being drawn up? Had she enough influence to have the odd name added to that list? Especially if the Manager wanted there to be a random element about it?

No. Lil Tasker was a Cockney housewife with threadbare armpits in her only outdoor coat. She had had money from the Manager in the normal way of underworld insurance while her husband had been absent. All that money above the subsistence margin had gone to Jackie. Lil was even now helping to finance the fancy-dress ball that was founding the thesis on sub-cultures.

And Jackie came out of her bedroom attired to perfection for the harem, even to a matching headcloth that could be pulled across her face if purdah appeared to be called for.

Lil Tasker snorted. Doubtless she took an earthy view of post-graduate research.

'Have you got transport, Simon?'

It was the first time Jackie had used his Christian name in her mother's presence. Kenworthy did not turn to see what effect it had on the older woman; the movement would have been too obvious.

'Nothing more exotic than a Cortina, I'm afraid.'

'Which way are you going?'

'I'd thought of the Mile End Road, Tower Bridge and the Elephant—'

'Pity. I'm wanting Bayswater.'

'It's on my way,' Kenworthy said.

They scarcely talked at all until he had them out in moving traffic.

'Mum's taking it harder than she shows. I don't know whether I'm doing the right thing, pulling her leg, trying to take her out of herself.'

'Were you pulling her leg about Dave Rowbotham?'

'Of course I was! Oh God, you coppers! It isn't safe to open one's mouth, is it?'

'But she does—did—know him?'

'As I say, Oh God, you coppers! I've given you a right old rat to chew, haven't I? She knew him as one of Dad's less desirable friends. You know what level that puts him on.'

'But that business of getting you out to the cinema? Did it happen, or didn't it?'

'Look, I'm sorry I ever loosed this off.'

'But for the record—'

'Making a record of me, are you?'

'You know what I mean.'

'Yes. It happened twice. But it was only because they wanted to talk about things that weren't for little pitchers' ears. Believe it or not, there were things about my father that I wasn't supposed to know when I was a kid. Uncle Dave met men who'd just come out of places where Dad was: Wandsworth or the Scrubs. He had news. Sometimes there were little commissions to be done, messages to be passed.'

She said it coldly, as a necessary explanation. When she had finished, she turned her head and kept her eyes fixed out of the window. Kenworthy regretted the turn that he had let the conversation take. He'd been behaving too like the copper of old. It was in his bloodstream. He'd lost ground with Jackie Tasker that he'd be lucky to make up again.

For what purpose had the Manager grubstaked her to a degree in criminology? There were mind-blowing unknowns. He started on an artificial topic, anything to re-establish rapport.

'This work of yours on sub-cultures. Has it taught you anything?'

'That people like dressing up.'

'Including yourself?'

'It's been fun. I'm going to miss it. It's nearly through. I start next week to see what I can get on paper.'

'For a Doctorate? Dr Tasker—it sounds good.'

But that was not a thought to wheedle her with. She turned to the window again.

'I owe you an apology,' he said.

'I don't see it.'

'For having the soul of a policeman. For letting my mind dwell on very remote possibilities.'

'You're entitled to.'

'I asked you once why you opted for criminology.'

'And I told you: to try to understand.'

'And do you understand – why people become criminals?'

'Wrong question,' she said. 'The basic problem is why other people don't.'

'Why don't they?'

'Some are scared. Most are indoctrinated.'

'So why aren't the villains indoctrinated?'

'Because that sort of indoctrination is an offshoot of privilege.'

'So basically your solutions are political?'

'I have no solutions. I'm not a reformer. I just want to know why.'

'And when you do know, you'll do nothing about it?'

But she changed the subject abruptly.

'Simon – are you going to start persecuting my mother?'

'Why should I?'

'Because you now have two points of contact that you think relate her to your hypothetical Manager: my father and Dave Rowbotham. I don't suppose we shall see you in Branwell House again, but you'll be making your report, won't you? And that will bring strangers round. If you knew how far-fetched the thought is, that my mother –'

'Jackie, if I were to make a report on your mother in my present state of confusion, they'd think I was mad.'

'But you obviously won't let Dave Rowbotham drop. You'll have to pursue him.'

'If I made you a promise, it wouldn't impress you – and your opinion of me would go down another two points.'

She had no reply to that. She did not speak again till they were west of King's Cross.

'Simon, I hated you when I was a kid. I hated you when

I first came to see you a few weeks ago. I'm trying not to have to hate you now—because you're doing a job that has to be done. And we Taskers have got to suffer through you—again!'

'That's because the Tasker indoctrination was never of the privileged kind.'

'No. It's because a little girl didn't like losing her father for months and years at a time. She didn't like other girls knowing where he'd gone. She didn't like the neighbours' smarmy looks. She didn't like their sham sympathy. And now, if my mother is going to be plagued—'

'Square one,' he said. 'Let's talk about something else. What sub-culture is it tonight? Real Mohammedans?'

'We're hoping to meet a few. Really, this stuff I've got on is quite a fashion. It just happens that the bunch I'm going to is following the mode for its own reasons. It's always better over the wall: let's look over the wall. They're keen on integration.'

She laughed cynically.

'Isn't it odd how people who have these big ideas are always defective in their own right? There are groups who are dead nuts for the salvation of Bangladesh. Others want to irrigate Ethiopia and Chad. They want to stop laboratory rats from being given cancers. But they can't stop themselves from smoking. They can't organize their own affairs, even at family level.'

'And you've got some real Arabs coming along? Or Pakistanis?'

'If they show.'

'Ah well—if one of them's a Persian, called Saroyah—half Persian, to be more accurate—you might let me know.'

He did not know why he said that: the need for inconsequential talk, the fact that mention of Middle East types had brought only one thing to the top of his mind. But the effect on Jackie was astonishing. She turned to look at him and spoke with highly dramatic deliberation.

'Say—that—again!'

'Loose talk, Jackie. I just mentioned a half-Iranian by the name of Saroyah.'

"What do you know about her?'

'*Quid pro quo*, Jackie.'

But Jackie shook her head.

'No deal. Not till I've done some asking around.'

'She's something to do with tonight's meeting?'

'Nothing at all.'

'But it's someone you know? It could be a coincidence—'

'No it isn't. We've been talking about what we've been talking about, and you come out with her name. That isn't a coincidence. I wish you'd tell me—'

'It has to be a frank exchange or nothing.'

'Then it's nothing—for now. But I'll be in touch. Incidentally, she's not Persian—not half, quarter or tenth. But I expect you know that. She has the look about her, and she cashes in on it. A London sparrow—I'll come back to you on this. There's something I need to check first.'

'We ought to have a deadline. This could be vital.'

'Trust me.'

'You haven't been trusting me this last half-hour.'

'Nothing is static, Simon. You don't know how near I am to coming down on your side.'

CHAPTER 14

No one would have thought of trying to get the Tophams and the Buntings on to one side of a sheet of paper, but the others on the list were easily condensed.

ROWBOTHAM, David: Aged 47. Domicile varies,

but seldom east of Stepney, north of Crouch End, west of Holloway or south of the river. Married 1955, separated '57. Domestic arrangements now casual-opportunist. Twelve convictions, seven custodial: petty larceny; taking a motorcycle without authority; being on enclosed premises; being a reputed thief, loitering about a warehouse with intent to commit an arrestable offence.

WYATT, John Simpson: ('Knacker')	Aged 23. Liverpudlian, two months served of first custodial sentence of six months: assisting in removal and disposal of stolen goods. Unmarried. Unemployed.
BOARDMAN, Albert:	Aged 29. Approved School. Borstal. Two convictions: robbery with violence (attacks on night watchmen).
CARLYON, William: (Billy)	Aged 28, married, three children. Born Falmouth, domiciled (latest) Leicester, taxi-driver. Second sentence of imprisonment. First: defilement of a girl under 16. Second: sexual intercourse with a woman he knew to be his half-sister.
HOUSTON, Angus Edward: ('Bomber')	Aged 26. Glaswegian, married, four children. Five con-

victions: aggravated assault; grievous bodily harm (twice); assault with intent to resist arrest; wounding with intent. *Houston has appeared before the Governor of Barlinnie Prison and insists that he will not accept release demanded by hostage-takers. Declares that he has no connection with this affair, and wishes to make that plain. Due for release in six weeks, claims that he has a good woman (not his wife) who will stand by him.*

MAYBURY, John Watkins: Aged 50, married, two grown-up children, whereabouts unknown; domiciled north London. Two custodial offences, separated by 15 years: obtaining pecuniary advantage by deception; destroying a record made for accounting purposes.

'We can add that he has his own teeth,' Kenworthy said. 'Not exactly the cream of the Manager's cream, I would think.'

By the fifth day after Waterlow's transfer to Grendon Underwood, he, Scales and Ulliatt had become a discernible team. They took to playing a good deal of Monopoly together. One or other of the two moles frequently managed to be within hearing distance, but no conversation was overheard that was not directly connected with the game in hand. It was noticeable that Waterlow played in a desultory fashion. He seemed bored, and had been known to truncate a game by demanding cash settlement of loans outstanding. The detectives considered the possibility that the terminology of the game was being used as a code, but it was not possible to isolate a meaningful pattern.

Bransby-Lowndes strolled into the office with his hands in his pockets. Just as he preferred to have no paper visible on his desk, so he seemed to like to move about the building as if he had no work on hand.

'How's it coming, Simon?' His use of slang was eclectic. It never seemed appropriate, either to himself or to the moment.

'Gaps are narrowing. But it's hard to know which one to watch.'

'The Home Secretary's becoming restive.'

'Can't help that.'

Kenworthy could not resist a shaft of disrespect that he knew Bransby-Lowndes would not like.

'Cabinet tomorrow. Try and find something new for him to say, even if it's trivial. Forrester's tied up on a dozen chores, and the word is that Hewitson's showing signs of fatigue. I don't like it, you know, Simon, this lull. I suppose the Manager knows it's going to take time for our lords and masters to digest this – but I'm dreading the first strike. I have a gut feeling that the Women's Institute is shortly going to be one member down.'

He idly picked up the carbon copy that was lying under Kenworthy's nose.

'So "Bomber" Houston doesn't want to be let out? Does that make him the most interesting of the bunch?'

Felicity Dainty, a minor poetess, was revelling in the salt of the dawn north-easterly on North Foreland, when she became aware of something not as it should be on the apron between the wire fence and the edge of the cliff: a bundle, a heap of old clothes, or maybe it was discarded bedding, was visible in patches behind a flourishing clump of mallow. It looked as if someone—there were people in the village these days who were quite capable of it—had tried to throw rubbish down on to the beach, and it had become entangled in the weeds. Felicity approached and saw with a momentary shock that it was not rubbish, but a female body—stockinged legs and broad-soled feet emerging from a hopsack skirt; a twin-set with which its wearer had been neutralizing fashion since the nineteen-thirties. Miss Dainty's belated imagism might not be to the taste of the general reader—or even of many editors—but that did not make her timorous, or even finicky. In particular, she was given to rushing headlong into any job which womankind was alleged to be inclined to shirk. She straddled the top wire, oblivious of inelegance, and paying no heed to how near she was to the edge of the soft and crumbling chalk.

She knelt alongside the body and her first impulse was to take the pulse at the left wrist. And not only was there a pulse to be felt, the touch of her fingers seemed to do something for the woman who was lying there. The body struggled to sit up, and Miss Dainty had to be firm to prevent the woman from trying to get to her feet and risk toppling over the side. Whoever she was, she was in poor fettle. She was also in some mental confusion, though visited by a strong desire to talk.

Miss Dainty directed, coaxed and eased her under the wire and suggested home, hot broth and a visit from the doctor.

'Exactly where are we?'

'The Thanet coast. Kent.'

'How did I get here?'

'That's something we can go into when we've got you

out of these wet things.'

'I've got to get back.'

'I've no doubt we shall manage that too, in good time. Back where?'

'Wherever I was brought from.'

'Where's that?'

'I don't know.'

The woman tottered, as if she had only partially thrown off the effects of some mind-clogging sedative.

'My house is only fifty yards across the cliff. Try not to talk yet. We'll sort everything out.'

But the loquacity of this foundling was unmanageable. She announced that she was Ann Teagle, Hon. Sec. of the Bishop's Fold Branch of the WI. It was all coming back to her now. She had felt pretty rotten after her goodnight cup of Ovaltine.

'I know what it is. They had to get rid of me—like they got rid of the vicar in that village down south. I was too much for them, you know. I was too much for them. But they need me there. Astringency, that's what they need. They're a lovely crowd, but some of them could easily weaken. And staunch though she is, I fear our President has a habit of getting men's backs up.'

She reeled again, seemed about to fall, and Felicity Dainty was so much taller than she was that it was difficult to walk alongside giving support.

'What part of the country were you in? Where were they keeping you imprisoned?'

'I don't know. None of us know. On a farm somewhere—in a filthy old granary that they've made into a dormitory. Some say it's the High Peak or the Yorkshire Dales, some say it's the Welsh Marches. Others think we may be quite near to civilization. Only two Elsans for the thirty of us—in the same room we eat and sleep in.'

They had arrived at Miss Dainty's house. The name-plate on the gate said 'Images'.

'But we've had them running in small circles. The one we call the Sergeant-Major, a man called Webbe: we've had him on his hands and knees. We *had* to have the floor scrubbed. We refuse to eat with cutlery that hasn't been properly washed and dried. We do not allow the guards to smoke in our presence, and we have at last succeeded in getting them to change into plimsolls for their night-shift. Oh, I can understand that they decided to get rid of me. But I've got to get back there. We're holding our normal monthly meeting this week. What day are we?'

'Thursday.'

'Blast! I shall miss it. Minnie Smith will write the minutes. She makes the book look like a reject from a kindergarten.'

Felicity Dainty rang the police before she rang the doctor.

Another of Hewitson's emissaries, Inspector Parrish, went to Morley Mortain. He visited both pubs: the Green Man, which is almost all public bar, and has no letting-rooms; and the Magpie, which is nearly all recently annexed restaurant, and which lets four B & B rooms, reserving one for guests unfit to drive home.

Did they keep a Visitors' Book? Yes, they did. People scrawled all over its columns, saying they had never had a better night's rest or a bigger breakfast. Parrish turned back the pages to two or three weeks before the Morley Mortain kidnapping. Harvey Vail, the landlord, leaned forward to see what he was finding.

'I'll be frank with you, Mr Vail. I'm looking for someone who came to case this village. Probably someone who only came here the once.'

'In that case, he probably won't have signed his real name, will he?' the landlord said, a rather sickeningly bright chap.

'But any little thing might help.'

Harvey Vail ran his own finger down the pages, practically taking the book out of the inspector's hands.

'Jack Blunt, travels in potato crisps and pork scratchings, comes once every two months. Terry Hawthorne, chemists' sundries, Bedford, Leighton Buzzard and Milton Keynes: standing order, Tuesday to Thursday, second week in each month. I suppose it's occurred to you that it could be a woman?'

There was a bounce about Vail that hit Parrish between the eyes; but he showed no reaction.

'Because here's one for you: Harriet Bateson. Opinion poll. No?'

'I'll take the details.'

And there was another who fitted the pattern. James Peacock: home address—probably false—a village in Hampshire. And in his case, the car registration number had been recorded in the appropriate column, though in a different hand, with a different ballpoint, from the remainder of the entry. What was more, it was an R registration, which coincided with Binney St Botolph: the man who had asked about the parish council and the coypus.

Parrish asked the landlord, 'Why didn't he write it in himself?'

'He left it blank. Not that I think it matters much to us, in a place like this, but there *is* a column for it, the way the book's printed. So I put it in for him. Pulling his leg, you know, ice-breaking, so to speak. I asked him if he'd forgotten it. Of course, I could see it through the window.'

'What kind of car?'

'Ford Escort. Daytona yellow.'

Ownership was traced as a matter of routine. Not Peacock. Not Hampshire. A man called Maurice Stephens, Birmingham—which fitted the LOJ prefix.

'Breakthrough!' Hewitson said, when the report came in.

'Breakthrough,' said Bransby-Lowndes, Forrester and Wright.

'I hope to God Hewitson's going to have the sense to give him rope,' Kenworthy said. 'At the risk of offending him, I've got to tell him. Raise him for me on the phone, Shiner.'

'We haven't made a list of anything since yesterday,' Kenworthy said. 'Pull a chair up, Shiner. Let's have another look at the cases that Special Crimes Squad left uncleared.'

May, 1976: Swiss Cottage. Working hours bank raid. £10,000 in used notes. Traffic hold-up in Kilburn High Street: Frank Tasker's funeral party.

October 1976: Whitworth Art Gallery, Manchester. No trace ever found of two Chardins and a Greuze. Question: crank private collector? Question: crime commissioned or speculative? South-bound road from Manchester blocked by multiple collision on cross-roads at Rusholme.

April, 1977: Bank vaults, Bristol, £137,000. Week-end tunnelling from neighbouring premises. No associated traffic jam. (No chase).

September, 1977: Working hours bank raid, Shepherd's Bush. £70,000. Lorry shed load of firewood in East Acton High Street.

June, 1978: Security van hi-jacked, A40 between High Wycombe and Nettlebed, Oxon. Driven openly after substitution of drivers. £150,000 in mint-new notes for bank delivery. None ever traced. No interference with traffic.

March, 1979: Wage-snatch, Fiveways, Birmingham. £100,000. Franky's second funeral, for which he landed in Cranston Green.

'Funny thing about that, Shiner. Characteristic of Franky. If he'd just stuck to a funeral, he might have got away with it. But he had to try something daft on the side. There were stolen furs on that cortege. That's what they did him for. Surely the Manager didn't know about that? He wouldn't want to double his risks, would he?'

'Unless he *wanted* Franky put away,' Wright said.

'He might have done at that. After all, the same thing happened at Kilburn, didn't it? And he made sure he never came out again.'

Then Kenworthy saw the answer.

'No, damn it, Shiner. This is the last word in finesse. Franky's jams were made to look as if they had to do with small-time crimes of Franky's own. That conceals connection with the Manager. No wonder a lot of money passed to the Taskers.'

Newsnight featured the Manager that night. Maxwell Durren and Christopher Medlock were the contrasting experts. Kenworthy and Elspeth watched, Elspeth in her dressing-gown.

And the country's most fashionable crime reporter had a bloody nerve. Called upon for the preamble, he brought out almost word for word the line that Kenworthy had taken with the Crime Writers, though he had sat through that with a sneer on his lips. He talked about superstition among the criminal classes. So far, so innocuous. But then he went on to say that managerial crime was usually too clever for such weaknesses. It hardly came under the heading of superstition, but there were, none the less, certain repetitions of style. There was a common link among some of the crimes they were here to talk about tonight. He went on to talk about a slow-moving funeral that had delayed three divisional patrol-cars in Kilburn, while £10,000 was being lifted in Swiss Cottage. He spoke of a concertina collision in Rusholme, Manchester, just after a car had got away from the Whitworth gallery.

'I'm not saying that these traffic hold-ups were a decisive factor. But in the Manchester case, the getaway gained a seven-minute start. That's roughly five and a half miles through a built-up area – which would make a change of car very much easier. And funerals seem to have been a popular way of slowing circulation down –'

Kenworthy swore under his breath. This was irresponsible bean-spilling. True, Durren lived by spilling beans; it was bloody remarkable where he found them all. If Hewitson were watching this, he'd burst a blood vessel. This wasn't playing the game with Hewitson at all.

'Are there any other common features about these traffic jams?' the presenter asked.

'There are.'

Kenworthy waited for it: Franky's name had to come out. But there were limits, even for Durren.

'There are. But in all fairness, it wouldn't do to reveal them at the present moment.'

'And do the police know about them?'

'One would like to hope so. But one is never surprised by surprises.'

Snide bastard. The presenter turned to Medlock.

'Have you anything to add on this score?'

Medlock looked sour; he hated Durren's guts.

'I know the case that Durren is talking about. I agree with him that it wouldn't do to compromise a line that the police may be following.'

'You're a man, Mr Medlock, who has built up over the years an encyclopedic knowledge of the professional criminal, his habits and outlook. I hope I'm not giving you an invidious image –'

The presenter smiled, but Medlock didn't; he was not a

smiling man.

'I'd like to ask you one or two operational questions—if I may call them that.'

Medlock did not even nod for him to continue.

'It seems to me, as a layman, that in theory an organization like the Manager's must be too big to work. I mean, it must be an army, mustn't it? And when you start talking about armies, you're dealing with forces that aren't easy to handle. Armies need discipline; and the sort of people you'd have in this army don't care for discipline. You need your own back-up welfare state. One man's disloyalty—one man's jealousy—one man's stupidity—could jeopardize the entire force. So?'

'I disagree.'

Medlock's tone was dry. He was intolerant of anyone who did not spontaneously share his point of view.

'I have put myself into the position of this so-called Manager. Incidentally, the term Manager is in itself absurd: the man is a proprietor. And I work it out that I could do everything that is attributed to him with a force no larger than twenty-four. Even that would be an extravagance. Given the right kind of chief of staff, I believe I could operate with a round dozen. Quality is what matters, not the size of the team. Of course, part-timers could be put on for special occasions. They need have only the vaguest idea of what they're doing. Certainly they wouldn't know who they were working for.'

'Would you like to be more specific about your theoretical set-up, Mr Medlock?'

'I would have to have an impeccable deputy. Someone to manage a false front for my finances: the clerical staff would not need to know what was going on. There has to be management of real estate: a house in Wiltshire has to be acquired—no problem. I would need a few general operatives and strong men when aggression was called for: say ten good men in all. I don't know how the domestic staff in Wiltshire was managed—but from all reports it sounds like illegal immigrants, operating under blackmail.'

'You really have got it taped, haven't you Medlock?' Durren said, and fixed the MP with a smile beautifully calculated to rile him. Then he turned to their presenter.

'So how much further do we have to look for the Manager himself? Here we have a man whose legal practice naturally brings the cream of the professionals to him. A man who has his own team of book-keepers who could be doubling up on other things. A man who could control the false front of a bent estate agency as if it were part of his everyday business. A man much loved by working women in working streets, because of his readiness to help their husbands in trouble. A man who can rub shoulders equally well with university graduates—'

Medlock could not take a joke. The presenter could not make up his mind how loaded the joke was. The producer at his window must have been gesticulating like a tick-tack man.

'Well, it's a good thing, Mr Durren, that we know when not to take you seriously. Thank you, gentlemen—'

The phone rang within minutes of the end of the programme: Jackie Tasker.

'Did you see *Newsnight*?'

'Hilarious.'

'You think so? Working women and graduates—'

'I wouldn't let that worry you.'

'It isn't that, anyway. I must see you. May I come over tonight?'

'What's it about?'

But she did not want to give a direct answer to that, was silent for seconds.

'Maybe you'd rather not be bothered,' she said at last.

'Past your bedtime, perhaps.'

'No. Come by all means. How are you going to get here? South-east is wearisome at this time of night.'

'I'll find my way.'

'I'll come in for you. Liverpool Street, corner of Bishopsgate. But come prepared to stay the rest of the night. I'd rather not have a double journey.'

There was another pause, then 'Can do,' she said. 'Good of you. Sorry if I sounded touchy. I *am* touchy. I have reason to be.'

He picked her up at an otherwise deserted bus-stop, wearing jeans—clean ones—and sandals, with off-white turtle-neck top. Her hair was neat, close-cropped, but she needed more of it for the size of her head. He drove them by Gracechurch Street to London Bridge, out through Southwark. There was always a special kind of emptiness about London street-lit late at night.

'Durren was pushing it,' Kenworthy said.

'I'm not particularly bothered about what those two said.'

'But your father always went to Medlock when he was in trouble, didn't he?'

'That doesn't put him in a minority of one. Though it strikes me now how often my mother was round at his office, when my father was away. I simply thought as a child that it was the normal thing to keep in touch with your solicitor when your husband is in gaol. I know plenty of people now who don't. It's my mother I'm worried about.'

Kenworthy waited. It was better for this to take its natural course and rhythm.

'And do you know—when I got home late one afternoon last week, I found Maxwell Durren in the flat? I know he has his enquiries to make—but I've never connected him with our kind of slumming. He was ostensibly digging into Dad's background for one of his features.'

'You say ostensibly—surely a fairly obvious thing for him to do?'

'Oh, Durren's so devious. Everything he does is ostensible. And they were getting on famously. But that's not what's upset me.'

She was being honest about herself. She was rattled. There was even a nervousness in her speech.

'It's Mother. And the starting-point's Dave Rowbotham. After the other night, I waited my chance to have another go at her about Uncle Dave. And this time, believe it or not, she made no bones about it: there had been something between him and her while Dad was away. It's the first time in my life I've ever heard her carry on about my father: what a cretin he always was. How she's had a lifetime of being kept short. Well: she was on the Manager's payroll, so she never was short. And *I* haven't been kept short—'

They were held up by a temporary traffic-light, so long-winded without other traffic in sight that Kenworthy was tempted to drive over it. He waited.

'But it wasn't that that peeved me. I dare say that most of what she said about Dad was true—except that she was forgetting his good points—what fun he could be—his common decency. And do you know what she said to me? She asked me if I wasn't old enough to know that there are some things a woman can't stand to be deprived of for ever. The thought of Dave Rowbotham—My God, if I had to fall back on the likes of him, I'd consider that a deprivation in itself. Oh, I know I'm the generation that's permissive if ever one was. If anyone ought to be beyond caring about into-bed-out-of-bed, I ought. There no sort of consistency in thinking it's different, just because it's your Mum. But I'm disgusted, Simon. Not least of all with myself for being so bloody sentimental.'

Kenworthy struck into a cross-street route that many a London taxi-driver would not have thought of.

'I'm sure it's all been a very unpleasant shock for you.'

'But that's not the worst of it. Don't you see how deeply this involves my mother in what's been going on?'

'No—I don't see that, to be frank. Do you mean because of this carry-on with Rowbotham? The only thing that connects Rowbotham with the Manager is that he's on this list of demanded releases. So are a number of other people—and there's a strong whiff of red herring about it. Rowbotham himself is gutter-bottom inept. What use would a man like that be to the Manager? If the Manager had had to rely on the likes of Rowbotham, he'd have been rumbled years ago.'

'I don't agree, Simon. So Rowbotham couldn't whip an apple off a coster's barrow without doing time for it. He's been inside God knows how many times. But doesn't that give him a special sort of cover? I can tell you what Rowbotham's job was—and it had nothing to do with the penny-trash nickings he was always in trouble for. What is it Shakespeare says? *This man is wise enough to play the fool*—if he's paid enough for it. Rowbotham's job's been collating and passing on news from and into gaols. Ninety per cent of his ordinary conversation is about what's going on on what landing in which cooler. It's important, you know, is visiting day. It isn't just a bored-looking screw trying to make sense of the crap that's being talked. It's a message from Billy in E6 to Mike and Charlie in the Feathers at Streatham. It's some poor devil in the prison kitchen being told that his wife's on the batter. It's Nick Howard being asked for the loan of his safe-breaking holdall: and where does he keep it?'

'OK. Understandable. Has to happen. But need it make Rowbotham more than an amateur?'

'Dave's always been one of Medlock's regular clients.'

'If Medlock's the Manager, he still isn't going to employ every oil-rag that his firm has ever defended, is he? He said on the air just now, he could do the job with a squad of ten.'

'I've been saving up the body-blow till last,' Jackie said. 'Haven't you noticed how like a woman I am, when it comes to dramatizing?'

But they were arriving at the Kenworthys' home now, Elspeth dozing on the settee. She was quickly offering hot drinks or something more sharpening, producing sandwiches she had cut.

'I suppose you've already covered everything in the car,' she said.

Kenworthy summarized the girl's fears in a few sentences.

'But she was just about to tell me the big one—'

'Saroyah,' she said.

'Oh yes—we had an agreement about her, didn't we?'

'That will wait. I know Saroyah. Have known her for years. Not exactly a family friend. But we knew her through Dave Rowbotham. She's some distant cousin of his. And she's been to our flat within the last week.'

She looked at Kenworthy to assess the effect of this. He seemed to be taking it casually.

'Her name isn't Saroyah. It's Sarah—Sally—Megson. She's a good-looking girl, with a dark-skinned, Mediterranean look. She could be a throwback—but in that case it goes back several generations. She's not half-Persian, though that's what she gives herself out to be—complete with the *Saroyah*. She's a prostitute, one of six being run by a man called Perry in Haringey. She came to Mum because she's dead scared of something. I'm not taken into confidence, of course. As far as Mum is concerned, I'm still the kid who mustn't be told things. What I did gather was that Sally Megson wants to be cached away somewhere, and she came to my mother as if she hadn't got another friend in the world. Mind you, Mum is pretty knowledgeable—and known to be.'

'I'm beginning to see daylight,' Kenworthy said. 'What sort of level is she on in Haringey?'

'That I can't tell you. I think the expression is, she knows her stuff. I gather that the Middle East angle goes down big with some men. I don't see why it should.'

'So why waste her sweetness on the desert air of Haringey? Anyway, if it's the same Saroyah, she was borrowed from Haringey recently. She did a stint at Fosse House in Wiltshire, delighting the males of Morley Mortain.'

'Yes, well, if I were recruiting for Fosse House—'

'The one she appears to have delighted most of all was Pastor Saxby.'

'That figures. That was why her conversation with Mum sounded so grotesque. I don't know what else Pastor Saxby did to her—but in addition to all the rest, she's now got religion.'

CHAPTER 15

Bransby-Lowndes came back from the Home Office with the plan of campaign. He had asked neither Forrester nor Kenworthy for special briefing before he set out. Sooner or later, Forrester said, his spasms of going-it-alone were going to get the Faculty wound up. But he came back unable to hide a rare enthusiasm.

'Operation ACADEMY, under Superintendent Castle, seconded from Admin and Ops, and accountable to Hewitson. We're going to release them all, including the fellow in Glasgow who wants to stay where he is. He'll be pushed out of Barlinnie forcibly if necessary. And one of the biggest round-the-clock shadowing exercises ever mounted is going to account for every movement of every one of them.'

'I hope they know where they're going to get the

manpower,' Forrester said.

'And what's the Manager going to do next?' Kenworthy asked. 'Hi-jack the Girl Guides?'

'We fight the battle of the moment,' Bransby-Lowndes said. 'It's the only one that counts.'

'Rubbish!'

Bransby-Lowndes looked at Kenworthy without pleasure. He was unused to that sort of value-judgement.

'In the meantime,' he said, 'There's nothing to prevent you two from trying to live up to your reputations.'

The inspector and sergeant from Met Traffic stuck rigidly to their brief. They consulted the highways departments of Staffordshire and adjacent counties and made notes of three lots of roadblocks that no longer existed, but that had been obstructions on the night of the Women's Institute's wild drive. They waited in a badly-lit side-street in Hammerford, half way between Uttoxeter and Ashbourne, and pulled away from the traffic-lights at the precise time that the shouting women had been rushed away from the bantering drunks.

'Nought to forty-seven in fourteen seconds,' Inspector Ted Ashby said.

He had in front of him maps, a torch, a clipboard with branching schedules, a pocket calculator and two stop-watches. They had spent the whole day practising on roads of varying contour and activity. Sergeant Gordon Meldrum at the wheel was becoming very skilled at reacting to sudden calls for speed-change.

'Went down to twenty-eight here, then stopped dead for three seconds. This is where they were working on the frost-damaged shoulder. Single-file traffic. Something must have been coming head-on.'

Then a roundabout, five ways out of it, one of them very minor indeed.

'He took this at forty-eight. Can't have changed down.'

'Poor bloody passengers! Which one, then?'

'Go all round it. Let's look at them all.'

Even they couldn't do it at forty-eight.

'Second one,' Ashby said, the second time round. 'If he was well-placed on the crown, he could have taken it almost in a straight line. Push it up. Seventy-three fluttering to seventy-five.'

They thumped over a stretch of temporary surface.

'Rough ride the old biddies had.'

They came to a tight right-hand curve.

'Didn't he slow down for this one?'

'Not within four minutes of it.'

'If we do him for nothing else, we can get him for reckless.'

Ten minutes later they were negotiating the right-angles of a village street where there could be no co-ordination between a viable speed and the figures on Ashby's schedule.

'We're wrong.'

Ashby stopped one of his watches.

'Find somewhere to reverse and take us back to where the oblique left went off to Aldwark.'

Robert Harrington Bryce, BDS: not a word had been heard of the dentist since his strep throat had got him out of the surgery. It was assumed that he was well out of the country.

But that did not prevent enquiries from being made about him, and the portrait that had emerged was suggestively unsavoury, though without proven offences. Bryce had been trained at Manchester, a dental school of justly proud reputation. A lecturer in prosthetics remembered him with uninhibited distaste. Even as an entrant, he had been looked upon by the more conservative of his tutors as a doubtful quantity. He did not look like a potential dentist. If not actually unclean, he just could not help looking scruffy. And there had been a nasty little business during his first surgery practice. With one or two others, Bryce had laid his hands on a rather prim woman student—not for sexual assault, but to put her and keep her just lightly under on nitrous oxide. This often has the effect of releasing a person's libido, and the patient frequently says things that cause high amusement to bystanders of a certain mentality. Unfortunately, this young lady told her boy-friend about the incident, and there was a very unsettling disciplinary enquiry. Bryce's dental career was on the line, and he was saved only because two others who had been involved were worthy students who would have to have gone down with him.

Then, when he was doing a spell of hospital clinical work, he was suspected of being mixed up in a small but pernicious drug-chain—an internal fiddle over stocks of pethidine, a synthetic morphine substitute. Bryce was believed to be managing an outlet for addicts at a pub in Moss Side, and there was enough evidence for charges to be brought. But he was defended by out-of-town lawyers who confused the court with such a plethora of doubt that a conviction would have been unsafe. Faced with this acquittal, and unwilling for a breach with student power, there was nothing much that the university could do about Bryce. He qualified minimally, but there was enough exchange of confidences behind the scenes to make it very difficult for him to break into practice. He was the sort of young man, then, who was likely to end up as a part-timer with a partnership in Coventry who were known locally as The Butchers; the sort of practitioner who was even happy to put in a day or so a week in HM Prisons.

And, too, he was the sort of young man who was wide open to blackmail when the Manager wanted a specialist—

Hewitson put someone on looking into just what legal aid it was that had saved Bryce's skin in Moss Side.

*

'Fifty-seven, fifty-nine — thirty-eight on this corner. God! We've got this corner right. Do you know what, Gordon? For the last ten minutes, we've been covering this exactly as per schedule.'

Ten minutes ago, and for the quarter-hour previous to that, they had thought they were wrong again. But then, as Sergeant Meldrum had said with pious optimism, there was no real telling what contingencies the Bishop's Fold coach had struck: they might have had a spell behind a nocturnal tractor. And Ashby and Meldrum had themselves sweated cobs when a tanker had pulled out from a lay-by thirty yards ahead of them.

A cross-roads. The speed dropped to ten. So the coach had probably not gone across.

'Stop a minute, Gordon. I'll recce this on foot.'

Ashby came back satisfied.

'Left. Steep gradient, and he didn't get the needle up to twenty for three and a quarter minutes!'

They were now in a lane so narrow that brambles were scratching the windows on both sides. In less than four minutes they dropped to a gentler slope.

'Thirty, thirty-five, thirty-seven, forty-two. Then another steep rise. He went down to fifteen.'

And lower: because two minutes later they were creeping up round a blind, narrow hairpin.

'How big did you say this coach was, Forty-six seater? I don't know how he ever got it round here.'

'The answer is, he nearly didn't.'

This was where the record — on the coach's return journey too — showed a series of half a dozen stop-start-reverses.

'He had to edge his way.'

Even Meldrum only made it in three.

'About another two miles. And we're going to walk a lot of it. We've been lucky to meet no one so far.'

Meldrum parked nose outwards in the gateway to a plantation. It was wild country up here. Mild as it had been down on the lower slopes of Staffordshire, the wind was singing here, a whine in the telephone wires. Ashby had a phenomenal memory for maps.

'I know the place now.'

'Break-through,' Bransby-Lowndes, Forrester and Wright had said.

Swansea had given the yellow Escort owner's name as Maurice Stephens. Stephens might or might not be the James Peacock who had spent one night at the Magpie at Morley Mortain. It might or might not have been he who had talked to Ketteringham in Binney St Botolph.

But Hewitson was not going to let this one get away. He put two double teams on finding and shadowing Stephens. Once they had found him, they were not to let him go for a minute of the day. They were to find some way of reporting every two hours if possible, every three at the outside. Hewitson would be at the other end himself, except when actually and unavoidably asleep. They were not to approach Stephens in any way. If they saw him commit every crime in the manual, they were to let him get on with it. They were to know where he went, whom he talked to, whom he went to see. Hewitson and only Hewitson would tell them when to strike; when Hewitson knew all he needed to know.

The team left London, and for twenty-four hours the only news they passed was that they themselves were in motion. They could not find Stephens. One of them, Sergeant Dawson, had pushed a CND leaflet into every letter-box in the block where Stephens lived, and established that Stephens's flat was deserted. There was a car park under the block, and in it the yellow Ford, its numberplates precise. Stephens was away from home, perhaps in a different car. They could only wait for him to come back.

Sergeant Dawson's connection with nuclear disarmament became so well known to so high a proportion of the flat-dwellers that he had to be given a rest before he wanted or needed one.

Sergeant Berry went the rounds of the landings, enquiring here and there for a Mr Eric Walton.

Sergeant Barton conducted a survey into gas or electric cooking preferences.

Sergeant Mills, officially in charge of the syndicate, brought with him a bag of tools and pretended to be doing things to a lift that had been out of order for two months. It was an unhappy cover; he came in for frank abuse from every man, woman and child who came up or down the stairs.

It was on Sergeant Dawson's second tour that things started moving. Dawson had used a dirty raincoat and bobbed woollen hat to alter his image, and was now examining fire-extinguishers and hydrant-points. Stopping often to look through landing windows, he saw a 3-litre Rover reverse into a vacant parking-space. The man who got out of it came obliquely across towards the main entrance to the block. But as he passed the yellow Escort, he looked back at it, went to it, stooped and eased a bit of gravel out of a tread with a matchstick. Dawson studied him: a man in his thirties who put a lot of money into casual clothes: today a brushed denim suit. He looked intelligent, was clean-shaven, wore spectacles with thin metal rims. Dawson plunged into his tool-bag, had an exasperating minute while two schoolkids loitered on the landing, then raised Mills on his personal radio.

'I need another pair of hands, Harry. Fourth floor.'

Dawson transferred his attentions to the fire-appliances on Stephens's own landing. Berry came up, a casually passing stranger.

'About time somebody gave that lot the once-over.'

'Twin-carburettor Rover down there. You watch it. It's time I packed in.'

Faint sounds of late nineteen-fiftyish jazz came from behind Stephens's door; vintage Brubeck. He had been with it in his time; hadn't he moved on?

It was not till nearly seven that Stephens appeared again, in an electric blue suit that looked as if this were the first wearing. Berry stayed behind him, Barton even further behind, ready to leapfrog. Stephens picked up a date on the edge of a moneyed estate. She was waiting in a telephone kiosk, only pretending to phone, was into the Rover in a split second. Married woman? They drove out of town to a motel; pricey restaurant attached. Stephens had a suitcase for them in his boot. She was an expensively cheap woman, white nylon fur, DIY blonde, large triangular ear-rings that did nothing for her. And she looked bored; the sort of woman who'd even be bored by her dinner, would leave half of it on her plate. Just out for a big, gasping orgasm. Berry did not enter the motel. Tempting to find out all he could, but more necessary not to be spotted.

The couple were there for the night. Mills would pick them up in the morning. He had managed to chat to a neighbour about Stephens: not scientifically, no claim to be reliable, just anything that anyone had to say.

'Firm's car he drives, of course. He's in the right line of business, that boy.'

'What's that, then?'

'Sells home-computers to people who don't need them, don't really know what they're for, but feel they ought to have one. Then he flogs them follow-up programmes to make them seem worth while. Bugger for the women, he is.'

'Oh, aye?'

'Anytime, anywhere. Four different faces in one week I've seen him take home. But he isn't often home. Travels a lot.'

Next morning, Stephens was travelling again. His woman did not leave the motel with him. Mills was behind him. They left town towards the motorway. Mills correctly guessed south, and had Barton, Berry and Dawson on the move too.

Kenworthy led Wright to the top of the sea wall alongside the ebbtide Fenland river. The sun was shining, but a cutting east wind was blowing in from the Wash. The horizon was far off in a great circle all round them: four distant Perpendicular spires and one Norman tower; seagulls and dried bladder-wrack on the spring tide-line. Kenworthy and Wright had had a case out here, years ago. Shiner believed that it was nostalgia for this that had had Kenworthy whimsically insisting on coming here. He could surely not hope that they would achieve anything.

And when they got to the hedgebottom where that poor devil Saxby had been found putrefying, the reminders of the prime years became so strong that they were barely tolerable—even for Wright. Those were the times that wouldn't come again: one inspector, one sergeant, getting it all done under the pretence of mooning about, that half-step ahead of the locals that made it seem almost like a leg-pull.

They would find nothing here. With Hewitson pushing, every blade of grass that could be turned would have been turned. The detail in that lab report would go down in forensic history, yet here was Kenworthy looking down into the ditch as if they were first on the scene. As if the trippers had not messed up such of the original layout as remained. There were beer-cans and beer-can handles; ice-lolly sticks, old newspapers. People had come here to picnic within sight of the grubbed-out hedge where a labourer's first thought had been that Saxby's body was a dead deer.

'Why here, Shiner? Why here of all places?'

'Well—it's lonely enough.'

'Lonely? It's damned near inacessible. Except for that lane—'

Narrow, flinty, lined with orchards and brambles, the deserted by-road came up from the back of nowhere, stopped dead, gated, at the bottom of the grassy flood-bank.

'The path report said the body had been dragged a fair distance. Well: he must have brought it some of the way by car. He wouldn't have carried it two miles out of town on top of the bank. Therefore he came by that lane. Therefore he knew where he was bringing it. Ideal spot: hidden from view, and there can't be more than one or two people past here in a day. He knew of just this ditch. He wasn't toting a corpse about, looking for somewhere to put it.'

'Must have been here before,' Shiner said. 'Same as someone who looked over Morley and Binney.'

'Let's go for a walk.'

Kenworthy led the way down the bank and along the lane. The world seemed lost behind a curtain of peace and green vegetation, a hum of insects, a fragrance of growing apples, a dance of field poppies in the verges. Two hundred yards after they had left the river there was a cottage on their left, one of those small, slender, single cottages that stand out in the Fen landscape like the deck-houses of ships. But this one had been tarted up, its walls rendered and pink-washed, its leaded lights replaced by picture-windows—a smallholder's hovel transformed into a middle-class escape. But its garden was neglected: gooseberry bushes spaced between apple-trees, nothing cut back, nothing pruned for years, grass and nettles thigh-high.

'Shiner, he must have come past here with the corpse. People won't say they heard, you know. Nobody wants to be involved. They're afraid they might have to take time off work to give evidence.'

'Hewitson's boys will have asked. They'll have put pressure on.'

'Well, we'll ask again. We'll put things a different way. We'll get awkward, if need be.'

Kenworthy walked up the brick-laid garden path. A clump of carnations had reverted to something primitive in their evolution. A rose had gone back to briar. There was a bellpush, but it was immovable under paint. Kenworthy hammered on the wood.

'No one home.'

So they went the rounds, looked in at every window. A small home: downstairs only a living-room and scullery kitchen; but a very new Calor Gas cooker, a very large, battery-operated cassette-player, a buffet unit in oak, a *Playboy* magazine on an occasional table. In a shed was an almost new Merrytiller.

'Good intentions, at any rate. Bachelor establishment, do you reckon, Shiner?'

'Don't see any evidence one way or the other. Pity we can't take a look upstairs.'

Wright looked hopefully at Kenworthy. There had been times when the Old Man would not have been beyond that.

'Better not. Just our luck for somebody to come home. Let's look in the dustbin.'

There wasn't one. But poking about on a rubbish heap, old tins and cardboard packets, he brought out a pair of nylon tights gaping at the crotch.

'Might, of course, be a bachelor pad for all that.'

There was no garage, no outhouse that could have housed a car. But a dried-out oil patch on an area of flagstones bore witness to where one had stood.

'One wonders, Shiner. One wonders. We'll ask around—if we can find anyone to ask.'

The only living soul they came upon within half a mile

was an ageless hedger sitting in the verge with his legs in a ditch, slashing with a sickle.

'Hullo,' Kenworthy said. 'I didn't think anyone did this with his hands any more.'

'What you reckon I'm going to do it with, then—my feet?'

'I've seen some pretty murderous-looking machines up and down the countryside.'

'Ah! And ha' you seen the hedges when they've a-finished on 'em?'

The man shifted his legs and raised himself to his feet, reached for a tea-can from a wartime respirator haversack. Clearly he meant to make the most of an unexpected social call.

'Nothing's what it was,' Kenworthy said—a safe sentiment.

'That that een't.'

From here, Kenworthy managed to steer the conversation from modern agriculture, through modern youth and modern unrest to changes in the face of the countryside. And hence to the cottage along the lane.

'Ah! That'd be Mr Allen's.'

'Mr Allen?'

'Ah!'

For a dangerous moment it looked as if the man thought that that had exhausted the topic. Then he spat into the ditch.

'Put a fortune into it, he did. Said that was for weekends. Two-three year ago, that was. I don't suppose he've been here more than nine or ten times all told.'

The tea the hedger was drinking was stone-cold and rich dark orange in colour.

'And every time he come, he have a different woman with him. And a different motor-car.'

'You've talked to him, have you?'

'Time o' day!'

'What sort of man is he?'

'Een't young, Een't old. Don't stay in one spot more'n a day or two at a time, what I can make out. Ha' to do with these here computers, he say. Don't reckon with the bloody things myself. Had to wait three months for my Christmas bonus on the pension, on account of the computer.'

They moved back towards the river.

'There had to be planning permission for that bit of reconstruction, Shiner. Some builder must have done the job. Somebody must have paid him.'

'Plunging a bit, aren't we, Simon? I mean, we've nothing to go on but that he's seldom here, likes his oats and lives near where the body was found.'

'That'll do to go on with. It'll do no harm to ask a few more questions.'

Inspector Ashby and Sergeant Meldrum parked their car nose outwards in the gated entrance to a plantation. The whine of the wind in the telephone wires would have made a good accompaniment for a Hammer film. Ashby had a phenomenal memory for maps, and his talent had been honed up by the present exercise.

'I know where it's going to be,' he said. 'There's a farm on the top. But for that, this lane wouldn't exist.'

'God knows what farming anybody manages to do up here.'

'The short answer to that is how many farmhouses have been let fall down—or been bought as country homes. I think we shall find that this one hasn't been farmed for a good long time.'

They stopped at intervals to listen for anything untoward in the noises of the night. A vixen was yapping in the middle distance. Something upped and out of a clump of grasses close to them. Over a crest three miles away headlamps stabbed up into the sky and were lost again.

'Do we reckon to get right up to the place?' the sergeant asked.

'I don't reckon anything until we've been and seen. Especially what sort of guard they have.'

Ashby pulled Meldrum into the edge of the lane. They heard something ahead of them: feet, making no effort to conceal themselves; voices, not speaking a language that the detectives could identify. They kept still, and two men passed them in the darkness, their conversation energetic and incomprehensible.

'Arabic, do you think?' Meldrum asked. 'They thought they were Arabs on the Morley job, didn't they?'

'We'll draw our conclusions when we get there. But I'll tell you what, Gordon: I get a feeling sometimes—this is it. And we may have to play this with a bit of caution. We rush at nothing. And whatever we find, they mustn't know we've found it.'

They waited for the feet and voices to be well below them, and they stopped more and more often to try to assess the darkness: a baying hound a couple of valleys away, a gothic owl in a spinney.

'It can't be more than another quarter of a mile.'

'No. And from now on no more speech. This lot are not likely to be patient.'

The eternal descant in those wires; a diesel-hauled train, a very long way away; a weird sound from behind a drystone wall: Ashby and Meldrum, core-dyed Londoners, were slow to recognize the breathing of bullocks.

And then they were at a farm gate. Despite his own ban on talk, Ashby had to whisper.

'Watch for trip-wires, booby-traps.'

He ran his hand gingerly over the top rail of the gate, waited for something to happen. Nothing did.

'We shall get nowhere this way. Sooner or later, we've got to take a chance, just one—'

In fact, they had already taken it. In the yard beyond

the gate, a dog had either heard or scented them. They heard the links of its chain pay out to their extremity and it began to bark in fury. A door opened, and someone spoke to the animal, which refused to be quietened. There were new sounds from the chain as it was released.

'Go get them, Rajah!'

'Move quietly away from me,' Ashby whispered. 'He may not be able to jump the gate, but if he does, we'll present a double target.'

And then another sound added itself to the scenario of the night. From what appeared to be a large granary over one of the barns, concerted female voices struck up 'Jerusalem'.

At Grendon Underwood, Detective-Sergeant Jarman and Detective-Constable Jones were beginning to suffer a feeling familiar to the imprisoned: the haunting auto-suggestion—none the less terrifying for the fact that it was in their case unreasonable—that they had been forgotten. With cloak-and-dagger security ploys, and the co-operation of the Governor, they made their regular reports to Hewitson. No information travelled in the opposite direction. Their reports were not acknowledged. No messages came in for them. They would have given their ears to have been asked a supplementary question. Moreover, they were both married men with young families, and had tastes of their own in pub-corners, armchairs and front gardens.

So it was little compensation to them that they were getting to know Scales, Ulliatt and Waterlow in irrelevant detail.

Samuel Scales, three years for abuse of insurance, due for release in three months' time, could have passed himself off as suburban-decent in any commuter compartment. He was the sort of man who could read typewritten reports all the way home in the train and then face the greater menace of greenfly in his roses, and a daughter whose taste in boy-friends made him wonder where he had gone wrong.

Walter Ulliatt, two years for export of used cars to which he had no title, six months still to go, was a man on whom imprisonment did not seem to weigh. He had been known to say that he was not easily got down: one had to make the most of where one found oneself. Certainly there was no suggestion that Ulliatt's conscience kept him awake at night. He had a hearty guffaw, which he did not inhibit, even when he was clearly the only one laughing. He was by nature a joker, a maker of apple-pie beds, a sewer-up of the bottoms of his neighbours' pyjama trousers.

William Greenlees Waterlow, local government Mogul, salesman of planning permissions, allocator of favoured leaseholds, entrepreneur of desirable sales-sites, was the moody one of the three. Perhaps it was because he was still a year from the end of his sentence. He was the one who most rapidly tired of Monopoly, who declined to make up a solo four, who sat most often in corners with no other activity than thoughts which were evidently bringing him no pleasure. Perhaps Waterlow was the reason why the trio appeared, after about a fortnight's friendship, to be spending less and less time in each other's company.

But there came a day in July when they were sent to work together on a farm out along the main Aylesbury-Bicester Road: loading up logs from diseased elms that had been chain-sawed where they had been felled. DS Jarman and DC Jones were also detailed as members of this outside work-party.

It was a large farm, some thousand acres of flat fields, fronted by a handsome seventeenth-century house on the highway. The felled trees had either stood in clumps or been scattered singly in parkland fashion. It was a beautiful afternoon, and there must have been more than one Grendon Underwood resident who had the feeling that this sort of pastime had been regrettably missing from his previous life. Scales and Ulliatt were working in the same group. Waterlow was parted from them, loading a trailer that was running shuttle services between the work-points. Jarman and Jones had no alternative but to work as convincingly as anyone in the gangs.

A little before four in the afternoon they had a tea-break and the farmer's wife came out with a tray of pastries that was an absolute bonus. She had with her a man whom she was evidently showing the way, and whom she introduced to her husband, who had strolled over from some other chore. The newcomer was a man in his thirties, bright-looking, wearing spectacles with narrow metal rims and a brushed denim suit. The farmer listened briefly to what he had to say, then shook his head with obstinate finality. Jones was the nearer of the detectives to the couple, but was unable to hear what was said. He watched the man, and saw that as he walked away, he took a semi-circular detour which brought him round behind the trailer. Waterlow was sitting on the edge of it, dangling his legs and taking his refreshment alone: more and more he seemed to prefer to be outside the immediate perimeter of things. The stranger stopped and had a word or two with him—it could not have been more than an inconsequential exchange. But the farmer saw what was happening, and shouted from a distance of some thirty yards.

'You! Out! What do you think you're messing about at?'

'Who was he?' his wife asked. 'Did I do wrong to bring him out? He said he wanted to see you, asked for you by name—'

'Only another damned rep. Do-it-yourself anti-biotics—'

Jones and Jarman had that talent of the experienced policeman that is sometimes wrongly called intuition.

Actually, it is a subconscious distillation of all that they have ever absorbed. They did not understand this incident, but they knew that it was somehow vital.

CHAPTER 16

It took time for Kenworthy to get the sort of attention he needed in the county planning office. And that took him only a stage nearer to the identity of the man who had established his bachelor love-nest on the fen. The plans had been negotiated by an orthodox firm of architects operating from Nottingham. It took further time to contact them. The plans had been commissioned by Brittlebank Holdings, also of Nottingham. Brittlebank Holdings were to be found in the Companies Register. There were three directors, whose names were not reminiscent of anyone.

'Aliases or nominees,' Kenworthy told Wright.

They put out feelers and came fairly quickly on the builder who had done the work on the cottage. It was a small concern: a man, his son, and such labour as they needed for the job of the moment. They came from Spalding, which was not all that far away, though far enough to look curious. There were plenty of local builders, whose transport overheads would obviously have been lower. It made it look as if care had been taken to keep local personalities out of the job, especially since it did not seem to have been put out to tender.

'Not to my knowledge, anyway,' the builder said. 'This Holding Company came to me with their planning permission, simply asked for an estimate.'

'Just casually, like that?'

'Yes. I got the impression that the man was just passing through, saw my signboard. Of course, it was all ship-shape on paper before I started the work.'

'This man. What sort of man?'

'Betwen thirty and forty. Well dressed—not flashily, but didn't neglect himself. The woman he had waiting in the car, she was the flashy one—'

It was worth a telephone call to Hewitson. Things were coming together. 'What Holdings did you say?' Hewitson asked.

'Brittlebank.'

'Pity.'

'What's so sad about it?'

'I was hoping it would be the same crowd who negotiated the lease of Fosse House.'

'Who were they?'

'Fowler, Tankersley, Successors, of Rugby.'

'See who their directors are—or who they call themselves,' Kenworthy said.

Fowler, Tankersley, Successors, turned out to be a façade for the same trio as Brittlebank Holdings.

'Won't be long now, Shiner.'

The four who were shadowing the man they knew as Stephens had no difficulty in staying with him down the motorway. He drove up to the limit, but avoided infringements: clearly, any entanglement with patrols would not be convenient.

He came off the motorway at Crick, transferred to A5, then crossed country to Aylesbury. He stopped for a meal south of Towcester, and the detectives ate sandwiches in two lay-bys. If Stephens had spotted that he was being followed, this might be his chance to elude them. So two drove on a mile or two, and one dropped back, in case he turned round. By that means—and thanks to their personal radios—they were still with him round the Aylesbury ring-road. They saw him slow up near the gates of Grendon Underwood Prison. He stopped in the village and talked to people who were about. He went into the pub. Dawson was in the lead to follow him to the farm along the Bicester Road. With binoculars over the hedge he saw Stephens speak to Waterlow behind the trailer. It was perhaps a weakness of their staffwork that he did not know who Waterlow was, and was not aware that Jarman and Jones were on the scene.

It seemed that the passage of half a dozen words had justified his journey. Stephens came out of the farm, shortly studied his map, and then drove towards London, skirting Maidenhead. It quickly seemed likely that he was heading for Heathrow.

Mills now took duty himself, with Berry covering him and the other two in reserve. Stephens studied the flight-indicators, went to the British Airways booking desk and then carried his suitcase to the Zürich check-in. The eventuality that he might try to leave the UK had been forseen by Hewitson, and Mills had his orders. He went and booked two Zürich tickets on his credit card and beckoned to Berry. They let Stephens get ahead of them in the queue when the Zürich flight was called. The shuffle-through was poorly controlled and ill-mannered. But another announcement was barely intelligible over the speakers: the final call for some other flight—to Malaga. Rapidly, Stephens broke out of the queue and made for the Malaga embarkation-gate. Mills was held up by a crippled woman, Berry was fighting a scrum using holdalls as fenders. They were both too late. The girl on gate duty was shuffling her papers, listening to them stupidly, gracelessly. The platform was being swung away from the aircraft, already the 707 was running up its jets. The girl called a security officer. He listened and thumbed his radio. The plane was taxiing.

Mills did not enjoy ringing Hewitson. But if Hewitson was short with him, it was because the Chief Superintendent knew that the next ten minutes were vital. He had two and a half hours in which to get something discreet laid on at Malaga Airport.

'I've said it all along,' Kenworthy said. 'There's one gap that won't narrow. Why, why, why, was it necessary to kill Franky Tasker?'

'Because we were showing too much interest in him,' Wright said.

'We've said that before, too. But what were we supposed to be showing an interest *in*?'

'The identity of the Manager.'

'I doubt very much whether Franky knew that. If the Manager kept it from anybody, he'd surely keep it from Franky. Unless Franky had found out by accident—and would the manager know that?'

'Something else he knew,' Wright suggested.

'For example?'

'Where loot had been stashed?'

'They'd know he wouldn't tell us that. That's something he surely would save up for when he came out.'

'Perhaps they killed him to threaten someone else—to let it be seen how far they'd go.'

'Anybody close to the Manager already knows how far he'd go.'

'An internal squabble somewhere in the Manager's hierarchy?'

Kenworthy pursed his lips in a way that Wright remembered from time past. It was one of Kenworthy's luxuries—a little ham act to register his own wisdom.

'I think that may be nearer to the mark than we've been yet, Shiner.'

He produced a familiar instrument and attacked his pipe with it.

'But it doesn't bring us any nearer to knowing what it's all about. Lil Tasker will know, Shiner. Than that there is nothing more certain. Lil Tasker has known all along.'

'But Jackie hasn't—'

'No. Jackie hasn't. Shiner, I'm going to see Lil Tasker again. And don't take this amiss—I don't want you with me. This must be between Lil and me. I'll work better that way.'

One thought led to another. Wright knew the signs when Kenworthy was going into overdrive.

'In fact, while I'm there, there's another job you can do for me. We'll have Jackie called in for questioning. You can do it. Question her about anything you like—as long as you keep her away from home for the span of the evening. I've got a feeling that Lil isn't at her best when Jackie's about—and vice versa. They unsettle each other.'

When he saw what he had got on paper from her, Hewitson came to the conclusion that little Ann Teagle was one of the best witnesses he had come across in his career—not only for what she set out to tell, but also for the unwitting revelations. Of course, one had to adjust to the volubility. The first few paragraphs of a statement by Ann Teagle were not answers to questions. They were outpourings that had been bottled under pressure. It was like settling down in warm surf, and finding that one has plunged into a breaker.

Ann Teagle got to know people very quickly. She knew everything about everyone she observed—remembered it all—and claimed never to have been proved wrong in a first impression. There was no false modesty or self-doubt about her analyses. She did not obscure her opinions with qualifications or compromise. She was a direct thinker who came to clear-cut conclusions. She expressed those conclusions immediately, with swashbuckling honesty. Hewitson never found time to ask her opinions on art: but he felt pretty certain that she would regard pastel shades as mushy and evasive.

Consider her view of the man she had hit with her handbag: Webbe, the one the Institute had telephatically nick-named the Sergeant-Major.

'Do you know, when I hit him, I hurt him? I don't mean pain-hurt—I mean inside-hurt. He didn't expect it. I don't think he had ever been hit by a woman before.'

'He wasn't vindictive about it?'

'In a comic way. For days afterwards, whenever he saw me, he pretended to be frightened. He was our chief gaoler—but I cannot say that he treated us improperly. He was doing his best to be very proper indeed—as he saw it. He was forever reminding us that as long as we behaved ourselves—as he put it—we had nothing to fear.'

'And did you behave yourselves?'

'Of course not. That would have been letting the side down. We let them get away with nothing. We insisted on cleanliness. We made *them* scrub the granary floor. We took over the kitchen, which made extra difficulty for the guards.'

'How many guards were there?'

'It was hard to tell. I think about six. But some were on duty outside, and there may have been more than we saw.'

'What sort of men?'

'Toughs. But we had very little direct dealing with them.'

'Tell me about the domestic staff.'

'Slovenly. There was a cook, Italian, I think. Once we got organized, we only used him for washing up and peeling potatoes. Even then, he got in everybody's way. Then there was a man we called Khaki Campbell, because although he was some sort of Arab, he talked with a broad Scottish accent. Also, he walked like a duck. I think he was some sort of illegal immigrant. I think a number of them were. There was the Latchkey Kid. We called him that because he had a thing about keeping doors locked, even from one room to another. He was an

Arab too. But he said he wasn't. He said he was Tunisian. Then there was the Ayatollah. He was Iranian.'

'Just three general duty men?'

'That's right.'

'No women at all? No one concerned with special feminine angles?'

'There were thirty of us seeing to that.'

'And Sergeant-Major Webbe: did he have any difficulty in controlling this mixed bunch?'

'Not as much as he had in controlling us. None at all, in fact. His word was law as far as the Arabs were concerned. He had an absolute hold over them. But as far as we were concerned, he managed to keep us locked up, that was all.'

'Didn't he ever try to punish you for making a nuisance of yourselves?'

'Occasionally. He removed the fuse from the television plug once, when Mrs Nichols had taken his cigarettes while his back was turned. And he lost his temper sometimes. We really were too much for him – and the poor man was so anxious that nothing should go wrong. I mean, we could see how it was. He was clearly under strict orders that nothing should go wrong. "I really wish you would have a word with your ladies, Miss Teagle," he said to me once. "Try and get them to understand that only over my dead body would harm come to any of them." '

'You seem to have got on famously with him.'

'He fancied himself as a bit of a lady's man, Mr Hewitson. I did egg him on a bit.'

'Yet you were the one who was finally slung out and transported to Kent.'

'That was because I got altogether too much for him.'

'Any particular incident?'

'It was when I hid his teeth,' she said.

'I can see that that could be exasperating.'

'You see, we had to have some sort of bargaining

power. Men like Mr Webbe don't normally scrub floors. And I knew he would do anything to get them back. Not only to eat with, but because although they were only National Health Service teeth, he was a very vain man.'

'How did you get hold of them?'

'Oh, I didn't actually get hold of them.' She shuddered. 'They were in a glass at the side of his bed. I covered it with a cloth before I picked it up.'

'You went into his bedroom? Wasn't that a terrible risk?'

'It was a sort of loft bedroom, overlooking the granary. We made curtains for the windows and made him put them up.'

'But how did you get in yourself?'

'Simply went in.'

'You're lucky you didn't wake him up.'

'I did wake him up. He thought I was there for—well, you know what, Mr Hewitson. I said: he was a very vain man.'

Lil Tasker was watching a cliché-ridden situation comedy when Kenworthy called. She turned off the sound, but left the picture on. She looked tired—the look of a housewife whose day—and week—have been too much for her. And the sight of Kenworthy brought her no sunshine. With wretched resignation she let him follow her into the flat.

'What is it, Mr Kenworthy?'

'Let's not root about the edges. You know what this is about. Who is the Manager?'

'It isn't known, Mr Kenworthy.'

'But you must have had theories in your time.'

'And I stopped bothering about them years ago.'

'Didn't Franky have theories?'

'You can guess how wide of the mark they'd be.'

'For example?'

She looked at him with sour fatigue.

'Leave it, Mr Kenworthy.'

'Is it Christopher Medlock?'

'Christopher Medlock can only talk. The Manager has to *do* things.'

'Maxwell Durren?'

'I only met him once in my life, and that was when he came sneaking for information the other night. I don't hold with any of this. I told you the other day, I want out of it. I don't know why I'm bothering to talk to you now. But I know one thing. The Manager, whoever he is, needs loyalty. Who'd be loyal to Maxwell Durren?'

'Loyalty can be bought, Lil.'

'Do you really think that, Mr Kenworthy? You can hire loyalty for money—perhaps for the odd job or two—but the Manager needs something long-lasting. Maxwell Durren could get any man's back up in five minutes. If he were the Manager, somebody would have shopped him years ago.'

'Well—somebody bought Franky's services—and never welshed on a payment, did he?'

'If I'd my time over again, I'd not touch a penny of it. Not that a penny ever went through my purse unless I was skint. I put it all by for Jackie.'

'Good for you.'

'And wouldn't do that again, either, if I'd known what it was going to turn her into.'

'You mean all this weird clobber she's been wearing. I wouldn't let that worry you.'

'Not that. That's just making an exhibition of herself. Any excuse—thesis or no thesis. No; you don't know what I have to put up with. You don't know how it hurts, Mr Kenworthy.'

'Do you mean you're afraid she's being turned into a Manageress? Are they grooming her for that?'

'Definitely not. If I thought that, I'd have killed her the

day she set out for that university.'

'You must have wondered. The Manager has strengths of his own. Blackmail can take many forms.'

'Jackie's not a bad girl, Mr Kenworthy—not that sort of bad girl.'

No. Maybe the only trouble between Lil and Jackie was that of any wilful woman with a twenty-two-year-old unmarried daughter living with her.

'She was upset by what you told her about Dave Rowbotham,' Kenworthy said.

'I meant her to be. It's high time she was upset. It's high time she stopped taking all sorts of things for granted. You don't think there was any truth in what I told her, do you? You don't think if I was pushed that way, I'd ever have turned to Dave Rowbotham for it? You don't think I'd ever *be* pushed that way? It just came out of me, when she started nagging me. I wanted to disgust her. There are times when I wish I could destroy everything that's ever been.'

That was as near to philosophy as Lil Tasker was ever likely to come: a retreat into nihilism—a practical expression of death-wish.

'But you did see quite a bit of Rowbotham from time to time—while Franky was away?'

'Of course I did. Dave's the best man I've ever known at getting messages in and out of gaols. It's a hobby with him. He hangs about in pubs and cafés on visiting days. He gets people to ask questions for him, he collects the answers. He talks to men who've just come out. He talks to screws off duty. And you don't know this, Mr Kenworthy—you've never lived our kind of life, never had to—we *need* to know what's going on.'

'And is that the job that Dave Rowbotham does for the Manager—when he's available to do it?'

'I have no idea what anybody does for the Manager.'

'So who killed Franky, and why, Lil?'

'You're beginning to sicken me, Mr Kenworthy.'

'You must have tried to work it out.'

'I don't even care.'

'They thought Franky was going to tell me who the Manager was.'

'Franky didn't know that.'

'Then they thought Franky was going to grass.'

'First, Franky never was a grass. Second, he'd nothing to grass about.'

'Then he must have known where some loot was stashed away from one of their jobs.'

Lil Tasker was paper-pale. The chances were that this torturing repetition was going to crack her open in anger. And if that happened, it would be the end of this interview. But she controlled herself strenuously: it would probably be the last time she would have to talk to him.

'Mr Kenworthy, I know that's not true. Franky knew where nothing was. I made him swear an oath by the open window.'

Kenworthy allowed it to be seen that he was impressed. It was an ancient superstition, went back to the underworld of the Middle Ages. If a man swore an oath by an open window, then the Devil could come in and capture his soul. People like Franky and Lil perhaps didn't believe it: but they wouldn't infringe it, either.

'You made him swear—here?'

'With the Bible in his hand.'

'When was this?'

'Not long before he copped this last stretch.'

'Well, that's one thing I don't have to ask you again,' Kenworthy said. 'And what particular job was it that you were worried about? Which lot of loot was it?'

But here was one which Lil would never answer. The obstinacy in her features was such that Kenworthy knew it was not worth pressing it—even though it was a key question, leading to a key answer. Lil Tasker knew something. It was something that Lil Tasker had worked out for herself, not something she had been involved in. She knew that that knowledge was trouble. And she wanted no more share in trouble.

'One more thing, Lil: this girl who calls herself Saroyah: Sally Megson, isn't it?'

'That bitch of a Jackie – she can't keep her mouth shut about anything, can she? Sal's been in trouble enough. You'll not expect me to tell you where she is. That's a piece of knowledge I'll take to the grave with me if necessary.'

'I know that would be useless, Lil. I won't ask you. But there's a line of thought I'd like to put into your head. Because there are odd policemen up and down who might take it into their heads to come pressing you. And it's this: Sally Megson is now known as having worked for the Manager: she was at Morley Mortain. She's some sort of relative of Rowbotham, who may or not be a Manager's man. She comes to you when she wants a hideaway. You were married to a Manager's man. So where does that put you?'

Lil Tasker looked at him steadily.

'That's the way thought's running, is it?'

'Isn't it bound to?'

'So don't you have neighbours in your street?' she asked him.'I suppose you call it an Avenue, which is different. People don't even know who else lives in an Avenue, do they? So if a man's a Manager's man – or been a Manager's man – does that mean that he can't be something else too? Have we all got little labels on us, so that we can't be anything else but what some people call us? If a man's a Manager's man, and goes to gaol for stealing furs – does that mean he can't do a good turn to a friend's friend? Mr Kenworthy, I don't think you know how people live. You just think it's a pity that some of us do.'

'Not at all, Lil – '

But if he went on talking all night, he would get no further forward. The misery of Lil Tasker was somehow broader and deeper than one usually encountered. He put an end to the talk.

There was just one new line of thought that had come to him during the evening. He put through a call to try to retrieve Franky's dental record from Cranston Green.

A little more information had come on to the files about Bryce. Hewitson had asked for local enquiries about his friends, associates, habits and haunts—and nothing had come up that looked as if it were worth following through. But there were side-issues. Bryce seemed to be a man fated never quite to live up to the standards about him.

He was even a rotten dentist. In a previous practice he had been thrown out for a spectacular piece of negligence. The crown of a patient's tooth had snapped off during an attempted extraction, and instead of doing something about the root, Bryce had plugged it with amalgam and allowed the gum to heal over it. The senior partner had saved him from an Executive investigation by making an *ex gratia* payment. Bryce was lazy; not a caring man.

Then there was the receptionist who had left her job in his present practice because he would not learn that she did not want the passes that he made at her.

A wholly insensitive man.

It was judged uneconomical to send four men out to Spain. Mills and Berry went. They arrived in Malaga by an Iberia flight some four hours after their quarry had landed. But Hewitson had been lucky with Interpol and the Spanish Airport police had handled similar situations before—to their own advantage. The man known as Stephens—which it also said on his passport—was singled out for Customs search. Something dubious was found in his suitcase—the official was enigmatic about it—and

Stephens was set aside to wait under surveillance in an interview room while a senior investigating officer could be found to come and question him. When it comes to bureaucratic delays, the Spanish have a temperamental start on some other nationalities—and this time they were trying.

Stephens had been held up for three-quarters of an hour in baggage retrieval. Another half-hour had gone in moving about and queueing at Immigration. He was half an hour at the Customs table, an hour and a half awaiting further attention. They seemed to think that he was trying to import a narcotic substance concealed in a tube of hair-cream. Stephens was no fool. He could not think how it had happened—but he knew that somebody was on to him. Something else was even at this moment being arranged for him. His suspicions were not allayed when, another hour and a half later, the senior official came back from a consultation and quite casually appeared to be dropping the whole range of their suspicions. He was dismissed: without apology, without even innuendo of compensation.

When Stephens stepped out of the office, he looked round the concourse of the airport to see whom he was lumbered with, somebody on his heels. He glanced up at the Arrivals indicator: the London flight from which Mills and Berry had landed was still on the list. Somewhere among the jostlers, the incoming hordes for Torremolinos and Fuengirola, there was someone with no other purpose than to watch for him.

Stephens moved round to a car hire kiosk: he had not spent years in mobile staff-work without learning how to get elementary things laid on. He drove east out of Malaga, along the coast road, in the little orange saloon, keeping a close eye on his mirror. El Pal, Chilches, Almayate—the traffic began to thin out. He dropped to a leisurely speed, allowed himself to be overtaken by a clanking cement-mixer that had been in his sight so long that it was beginning to trouble him. He let it get ahead, himself turned left and north at Torrox, climbed narrow and lonely hill roads. There was a primeval beauty in the landscape, a sweep of blue distances, a scattering of white farms on the hillsides. But Stephens was not touched by landscape. He had a lot to do in a little time.

Among other talents, Stephens was a specialist in safe-houses. In Spain the cover for that had been easy. The agencies were used to expatriates who needed winter sunshine and cheap brandy. Of the two houses with which Stephens was concerned on the Costa del Sol, one was such an orthodox acquisition that it had actually been sublet a time or two to ordinary people for the sake of realism. It was a modern pastiche of a traditional Andalusian villa on the hills between Nerja and Maro. It was generally available for figures in Stephen's entourage who had got themselves into incidental trouble. That was where Bryce would be now. It was a staging-point from which he could hope to be moved on when something had been laid on for him. Something had to be laid on for him now. He had to be moved on to somewhere where no one need have anything to fear on his account. If Stephens had had his way, Bryce would never have had any place in the organization.

The second safe-house with which Stephens was concerned was not available for all and sundry. 'Las Cabras', in the hills above Torrox, was very remote. It had such a broken-down appearance that from a distance it might even have seemed to be a ruin. Inside, it was several times more comfortable than the cottage that Stephens had organized for himself in the Fens. Sometimes people had come here to do business with other people who were not thereafter seen again. Stephens had also sometimes stayed here with women. Well, he wasn't going to bed at all to-night, but tomorrow, when his work was done, he'd get himself organized.

He did not approach 'Las Cabras' until all the roads in sight had been deserted for so long that he convinced himself that he had not been followed. Then, ignoring the dust-sheets, he retrieved an Erboa automatic that had been laid away between joists with its barrel and mechanism well greased. With the security checks on every airport passenger these days, there had been no question of bringing a weapon out with him. He took a leisurely half-hour over cleaning the gun. Then he went into the yard, and after scanning all horizons, fired one experimental round at a lemon hanging from the lower branch of a tree. He smiled faintly as the fruit squelched. He had not lost his touch. One round had done for Saxby, and it would be preferable for one to do for Bryce.

The echoes of the shot died out in the surrounding hills. If anyone had heard it, they would assume that it was someone out after game. Somewhere an empty distance away, he heard the bells of a herd of pasturing goats. The sound held no magic for him.

'My God, Simon, next time you want me to entertain one of your young friends—'

'She gave you a rough time, did she?'

'She doesn't trust people, does she? She knew there was something phoney when I wanted to talk to her. It troubled her. And you don't get much out of Jackie when she's troubled.'

'So you—?'

'So I suddenly thought of something that's never occurred to me before. I told her the truth.'

'Better not let it become a habit.'

'I told her my job was to pin her down while you talked to her Mum.'

'That's when she went for your eye-sockets?'

'Oddly, no. Strangely enough, it seemed to settle her

down. A bright girl. She saw the sense of it at once. I think she was relieved that it was happening at last.'

'And what did you learn?'

'A lot—about Saroyah. She started thinking aloud—expounding a few theories of her own, no doubt hoping that I'd join in and let slip a few of our own ideas.'

'So you did join in.'

'We pooled a good deal of information. I've never been more inventive in my life. I got her talking about Saroyah. She knows where she is. She's been to see her. She worked it out from probability, she said. It was a question of knowing her own mother. If Lil Tasker advised the girl to go to ground, where would it be? Jackie narrowed it down to three possibilities—all in London. The old one about hiding in a crowd—plus the fact that where else does Lil Tasker know anything about but London? So Jackie moved around. Second time lucky—she found the kid. Wouldn't tell me where. And there was a limit to the pressure I could put on—I don't want you to think that I let Jackie call the tune, but—'

Wright pulled an odd face. He was not a young man any more—but he could still be surprised by things that would not have surprised Kenworthy.

'Well, that's just it, Simon. Saroyah—Sally Megson—is just that, just a kid. A cheap tart—a bit higher than bargain basement, maybe, because she has what they say it takes. She gets recruited into the Morley Mortain lark because she happens to be known by whoever's doing the recruiting. From her description, it looks to me very like the man that the WI called the Sergeant-Major.'

Wright seemed to think that there was too strong an element of coincidence about that.

'What's wrong with it?' Kenworthy asked. 'He's doing the recruiting; he knows her—'

'But surely an organization like the Manager's can do better than Sally Megson?'

'In what sense?'

'Someone more trustworthy.'

'They all trip up sooner or later, Shiner. We'd be out of business if they didn't.'

'Yes, but we've always given the Manager top rating. This looks as if his outfit's running down.'

'Could be that,' Kenworthy said, and fixed Wright with the theatrical knowing look that had marked watersheds in some of their cases together.

'I think that's a point to which we may not have given enough attention, Shiner—that the outfit might be running down.'

'Well, anyway, at the beginning of the Morley Mortain business, Pastor Saxby was spending long hours alone with Rita Lonsdale. Then either he tired of her, or she tired of him, or they had a massive row, and Saxby was out on a limb again. So Saroyah set out to see what she could do with him. And lo and behold—this is the bit that I find hard to believe—Saxby starts teaching her the message.'

'What's so odd about that? People have been known to get the message, Shiner. Look at the Sally Army. I've known some rough old cases brought by them to what they call the Mercy Seat. And they've stayed there. Been the making of them.'

'Yes, but Sal Megson—'

'You don't know Sally Megson. You've only heard of her. You only know what you think she might be like. Sentimental little soul, in all probability. And Saxby did have a way with people. He had his following—even in rural Beds. His method is emotional manhandling; I've heard it called emotional masturbation. But it clearly works with some, and the more sentimental they come, the easier meat for him.'

'It seems to have worked with Sally Megson. Jackie says she's still riding the rods on the Judgement Train. Nothing suited her but that she had to help Saxby escape from Fosse House. She wasn't in the confidence of the hierarchy, did not know that they were all going to be released the next day, anyway. She got the pair of them out—it wasn't too difficult. She'd had a good sub on this ploy, and she had enough money to look after their immediate expenses. They went off—to Southend of all places—on what seems to have been a mixture of dirty weekend and revivalist meeting. Then Saxby disappeared. Sally did not know how—and didn't know how she hadn't been picked up herself. She was distraught. Of course, the thought did occur that she might have offended him; he does seem to have had a nasty little habit of ticking her off for this, that and the other. She changed her hotel. After a day or two she sneaked back to the Smoke, didn't dare show herself in Haringey. A week or two later, when Saxby's body was found, she knew for sure what danger she was in. Her clever cousin Dave Rowbotham was away. She went to see Lil Tasker.'

'She's been lucky,' Kenworthy said.

'But why did Saxby have to be killed?'

'Because of what he might know. There'd been tight precautions against the hostages' finding out too much about what was going on. But don't forget that Saxby was in cahoots with Saroyah. She didn't know it all, either—but she knew more than he did. I'm sure that's it: he was killed, not for what they were certain he knew—but for what they were afraid he might know. He'd only got to be able to identify one of them to us—'

'You may be right. Failing any other explanation, I suppose you've got to be. But have we ever known the Manager take that sort of risk before? It sounds too unsubtle for him. Something's missing somewhere. The Manager's not what he was.'

'Or even possibly *who* he was, Shiner. Has that possibility occurred to you?'

*

The mobile cement-mixer was a standing device of the Spanish police. When Stephens turned north into the hills above Torrox, the thundering old vehicle dropped a passenger at the next Guardia barracks. The Spaniards had had a latent curiosity for some time about 'Las Cabras', the furnished villa that had not been visited for years—and that could be mistaken for a ruin at a distance. This late afternoon they guessed, gambled—and won.

They worked a man up into the hills, no farther by car than would bring the sound of its engine within sound of the villa. His binoculars picked up the orange of the hired car in the yard. Mills and Berry waited at the bottom of the hill in Torrox, sipping weak beer as slowly as was physically possible at a pavement table. Sooner or later, Stephens might come back down to the main road. If he chose some more devious route, the Guardia were confident they could pick him up in the hills.

Outside the gate of the Derbyshire farm, Sergeant Meldrum moved down the hill, away from his inspector, at the approach of the dog. The next moment would answer a critical question: could the animal jump the gate?

It could; and it did—and presented with two targets, it went for the one on the move: Meldrum. Ashby picked up a half-brick and hurled it at short distance, with all the violence he could summon. It was a good shot, catching the animal at the base of the skull, but not with enough force to stun it. It reeled, righted itself—and turned on its attacker.

But up at the farmhouse now there was unco-ordinated activity. The Sergeant-Major and all his guards were out of the house. There was shouting of orders, counter-orders, and a vain attempt to see whether orders were being carried out. If anyone had wanted a sign that the machinery of the Manager was running down, the evidence was abundantly here. Basically, it was the discipline of years that had broken down. Ann Teagle had been basically right about Sergeant-Major Webbe: he could not cope. Still less could he cope when he realized that the Women's Institute were out of the house and all round him, with all sorts of inelegant cardigans thrown about their *déshabillée* and armed with anything seemingly suitable that came to hand as they passed through the kitchen.

Sergeant Meldrum came back up the slope when the dog turned on Ashby. This time it was the sergeant who threw stones and the dog, hurt, confused by the many voices, made menacing pretences of attack—but dared not come near enough to finish them off.

In fact Webbe and his minions escaped into the hills, not knowing by what manpower they were being raided. It took a day or two to round them up—but by then their support services had dissolved. The women were not all that easily convinced that Ashby and Meldrum were friends; it took about fifteen minutes in all for peace to settle.

In various of Her Majesty's Prisons, certain men had drawn their civilian clothes from store and had tried them on, ready to step through the gates the next morning. The Topham brothers and the Buntings (who were actually cousins) were yet to learn how sharply fashions had changed since the swinging years in which they had last been at liberty. Dave Rowbotham was amazed how much weight he had put on. 'Bomber' Houston was sitting naked in his cell, refusing to co-operate.

The next morning's news was broken at the cell-doors with degrees of tact that varied according to the moods and imaginations of the officers on duty.

'All right, Carlyon, you can get that lot off. Get into what suits you better. No fancy shirt for you today, my lad. Somebody's had a big change of mind.'

'Sorry, Maybury: order, counter-order, disorder. So as a special treat you can report to the kitchen for sink-duty.'

'You'll catch your death, Houston. Get your proper clobber on. Scrub round yesterday's orders. And you're up before the Governor at ten for refusing to comply with them.'

Mills and Berry had a relatively easy pursuit—late at night, along the precipitous corniches of the coast road—but with enough occasional traffic for them not to be suspect: and with Stephen's headlamps to guide them, they could afford to drop well behind.

Stephens left the highroad east of Nerja and went up to the safe-house that was an imitation of the ancient Andalusian pattern. Mills and Berry parked their car, too, and merged into shadows. Presently, Stephens came down the hill on foot with another man, whom he ushered down the cliff-gap entrance to a beach that the map called Burriana.

There are a large number of beaches labelled Burriana on the Spanish coastal map. Their tideline is a uniform ejection of old plastic containers, of rotting palm-roots, of discarded rope-soled sandals and split lengths of bamboo. But by partial moonlight, the debris tends no longer to dominate the scene. There is a silver scintillation where the waves cream over, a ceaseless gentle heaving of surf against shingle. The power of nature can be heard and felt at the back of the night. Perhaps that makes an appropriate backcloth for a man about to meet his death.

Mills and Berry were not in time to prevent it. That is one of the troubles about giving one's quarry his head. Sooner or later he may achieve what he set out to do. In this case it was to fire an Erboa automatic within inches of the nape of a man's neck. The same thing had happened to Saxby. Berry and Mills were too late to stop it, but they were in time to pin Stephen's arms to his sides as they waited to ambush him in the cliff-gap.

CHAPTER 17

Kenworthy received a Sunday morning visit at home from Maxwell Durren. Moreover, he arrived so soon after his phone-call that he had obviously made it from round not too many corners. He was in as affable a mood as he was capable of—though never able to throw off entirely his conviction of superiority. He must have been objectively aware of this, for this morning he did make some effort to suppress it. But it was not long before the normal Durren was breaking through.

'I've come to pick your brains, Kenworthy.'

'It's a change to be treated as if I have any.'

'Oh, come, come. You and I have never actually done battle.'

'I wonder why that is?' Kenworthy said. 'In any case, you must know that my connection with all this, tenuous as it is, is nevertheless protected by the Official Secrets Act. I was called in for second opinions, that's all.'

'So you know what all the first opinions are.'

'And, as I say—'

'Good God, man—you don't think I've come to pump you for indiscretions, do you? They've used you as a part-time consultant. You're also a civilian, a private citizen, with opinions of your own. You're entitled to express those opinions. Of course, I'm not going to quote—'

No; he wouldn't. Durren seldom quoted sources. He preferred to pass off other men's opinions as his own.

'I'll tell you what's on my mind,' he said. 'You can please yourself whether you say anything or not.'

'Thank you for advising me as to my rights.'

'Really, Kenworthy! It's this, anyway. I don't understand why those prisoners have not been released. All right: you've got the women out—or they got themselves out: jollity and "Jerusalem". You've got a few of the Manager's hoods. But what's the Manager going to do about it? Who are going to be the next bunch of hostages? Do you think he's going to accept this as defeat: when you still don't know who he is? Next time, is it going to be kid gloves—or piecemeal murder? It seems to me, if you'd let those chaps out—and mounted your famous operation ACADEMY to keep tabs on them—sooner or later you'd have been taken to where you ought to be wanting to go.'

'You'd have us let the Tophams and Buntings back into Soho?'

'OK—hang on to the Tophams and Buntings if you like. Nobody seriously believes that the Manager wanted them out. They were a blind—a cover for the one he was interested in. Let just a couple out: Rowbotham and Maybury. Isn't it the official belief that those were the two nearest the Manager?'

'You can quote an inspired source,' Kenworthy said, 'as saying that we don't think there's much danger now that the Manager has lost the second of his country residences. He can't go on pulling suitable properties out of the bag for ever.'

'That horse doesn't even start. You can keep hostages in the third-floor back.'

'Well, don't look at me as if I'm responsible,' Kenworthy said. 'This is not my decision. Not even a police decision. This is Government.'

'Would it be true to say that your colleagues—your former colleagues—are unhappy about it?'

'No, it wouldn't. But what's this sudden obsession with the truth? I never thought you cared.'

It was tempting to descend to childishness. Durren

made a fresh effort to be sweetly reasonable.

'Kenworthy, why treat the press as an enemy? Oh, I know that some of the lesser lights—'

'It's no good, Durren. I can't tell you what I don't know. And if I did know, I'd be barred from saying.'

No go. Durren had to see that it was no go. Kenworthy was not going to be dragged into it. They did not exactly part daggers drawn—except in so far as Durren's hilt was always half an inch above the scabbard.

Elspeth thought that Simon had behaved foolishly—she'd managed to listen in to the whole of the conversation. Now he'd be getting one of Durren's columns to himself in the not-too-distant future—and that was going to make him difficult to live with—among other things.

'What's more, I agree with him. There *will* be another rash of kidnappings.'

'Absolutely not.'

'You do exasperate me sometimes. How can you speak with such certainty about a thing like that?'

'Apparently you can. And the answer is because the Manager isn't interested in any of the men on that release list.'

Elspeth closed the door and came and stood in front of him.

'Simon—what do you know now?'

'Durren said that the Tophams and the Buntings were on the list as a blind. *I* say the whole list was a blind. I think that the Manager had already got what he wanted, and that everything but that was red herring. We had a pointer to it in something that Ann Teagle's Sergeant-Major let slip. The poor devil didn't know how to handle those women. They were his hopping-pot. If he could have got tough with them, as he did with the Norfolk bunch, he could have coped. But his brief here was that no harm was to come to anyone. And I was wrong—'

'Never!'

'I was wrong, Elspeth. I thought those North Country women were going to be killed off one by one as a more or less daily event. But detaining them was purely academic. They were there to obscure what the Manager had already fought for and won.'

'But what?'

'Well, he got mice introduced into Franky Tasker's cell for one thing.'

'Simon!'

'Elspeth, you didn't see Franky with those mice. This was a phobia. It was the sort of thing that can drive a man mad. Franky would have conceded a great deal to have been rid of those animals—rid of the smell alone.'

'But what good did that do the Manager?'

'I don't know. They're still dragging their feet in Cranston Green. I'm going to try to get out there tomorrow.'

'Well, it's not for me to talk about how many eggs you've got in how many baskets.'

'Because I've got spare eggs and spare baskets. Don't forget that the Norfolk hostages also got William Waterlow transferred to Grendon Underwood.'

Monday morning: and Forrester had three new files. He was to discover—strictly for information only—who really was fomenting industrial discontent in Peterborough. He was to try to trace to its source a rumour in Belfast. And he was to find out who was financing a family who were campaigning about a young thug injured when police charged a street riot.

And Bransby-Lowndes was busy: he actually had a piece of paper in his hand. It was Kenworthy's latest request to ask questions in Cranston Green.

'I don't know what you think you'll gain by it. I can see the Governor bringing a case for harassment.'

'Franky Tasker had dental attention—from Bryce—less

than a week before he died.'

'He didn't die of Novocaine poisoning.'

'No. According to his record card, they didn't use Novocaine. He had an abscess under a molar. There used to be an old wives' tale that local anæsthetic can't be relied on where there's an abscess. It may be absorbed in the abscess itself, and not affect the surrounding tissues. I don't know how true it is. It doesn't matter very much, anyway, because I don't believe that Franky had an abscess—or even a bad tooth.'

'What the hell are you on about?'

'I'm thinking that Franky was called to the surgery to be told that if he answered a certain question he'd be relieved of his mice. But the price was too high. Even Franky was prepared to stick the little buggers out.'

'So?'

'So Bryce put him under nitrous oxide—laughing gas—and got him to talk that way. There's a note about Bryce. He did that to a girl student at Manchester. When you put a patient lightly under, and put ideas into their minds—in other words, ask them questions—he'll answer them—oh, with a lot of bloody rubbish mixed up in it.'

'Simon, I know this is ingenious—'

'For God's sake!' Kenworthy was surprised at the rage that flared out of himself. 'For God's sake, Bransby-Lowndes, why will you people never accept facts because you don't find them orthodox? Bryce *did* give Franky Tasker nitrous oxide that day. It's noted on the card. And it was witnessed by a medical man. They have to take damned good care of these things these days—even in gaol. I need to talk to that doctor.'

'OK, but it's the last time you go there.'

Forrester threw down the third of the day's new files.

'I think I'll go with him.'

Bransby-Lowndes had so little faith in any of it that he did not oppose that. And Kenworthy's journey led to another tangle of wasted time. He cursed himself for not having checked. The doctor concerned—a young woman, not a man—had been moved; was at Maidstone. He found her at last, and she remembered the incident.

'I shouldn't think it funny, but it was. The patient was scared stiff of the extraction—kept saying it wasn't necessary. And the dentist was in hilarious mood: kept pulling his leg about some mice he was supposed to be keeping in his cell. I suppose it was all to take his mind off the surgery. And then when he got him under, he started asking him silly questions, pretending he was trying to find out for his own purposes where some loot had been hidden. The patient was funny. He kept saying £150,000 in new notes. Said they were in—'

Kenworthy returned to Whitehall, had a blinking and furious Bransby-Lowndes interrupted in committee, set a slip of typescript in front of him.

> *June, 1978:* Security-van hi-jacked, A40 between High Wycombe and Nettlebed, Oxon. Driven openly after substitution of drivers. £150,000 in mint-new notes for bank delivery. None ever traced. No interference with traffic.

'None were ever traced,' Kenworthy said, 'because the Manager knew the dangers of that. He was prepared to be patient—to wait a year or two, till the chances of a number-check receded. In effect, he did not mean to wait as long as he actually did. But in the meanwhile he was in gaol himself. And there was no interference with traffic, because with substitution of drivers, it was a considerable time before the theft was discovered. Besides, Franky Tasker—who normally looked after traffic diversions—was otherwise engaged that day. He was the one entrusted with getting the loot away. I'm hoping that what he said under laughing-gas is true, and that we shall find it in Branwell House—partly under the floorboards, but mostly inside the lagging of a water-tank. Oh, Franky: you should never have sworn to a lie with the window open—'

'I wish you wouldn't talk in such riddles, Kenworthy. What's all this about the Manager being in gaol?'

'William Greenlees Waterlow,' Kenworthy said. 'Came unstuck over that side of his business that had nothing to do with being the Manager. Got in the way of big insurance money and had to be taught a lesson. But he had a good team, when it was going. Stephens was a good man: property deals, safe-houses—ruthless dealing with men like Saxby. Bryce was a hit-man who wouldn't draw the line anywhere. Webbe—the so-called Sergeant-Major—must have been fairly low down in the pecking order in the vintage years. So was Frank Tasker. So was Dave Rowbotham: but he had his purposes, when it came to prison-message running. All very well. With Waterlow inside, the rump of the gang wanted to make a go of it without him, Stephens controlling, I would imagine. They did the Fiveways snatch—for which Franky landed inside. But it was classical managerial stuff—without the Manager.'

Kenworthy felt in four pockets for his pipe, eventually produced it.

'Enter Scales and Ulliatt, who've got to know quite a lot along the vine. They're going to be out and about before Waterlow is. They want to take over the rump of Waterlow's cadre—in association with Waterlow. In other words, no longer a Manager, but a triumvirate. Certain preliminaries are necessary. £150,000 that Franky Tasker could put his hands on for them. And, of course, they need to get Waterlow to Grendon Underwood for the planning stages. Waterlow didn't like the idea much; he even sulked out of Monopoly. And Ulliatt was the joker in the pack: he'd be the one who thought of the mice.'

'Snag!' Bransby-Lowndes said, a highlight of intelligence in his eyes. It was one of his moments for going through the surrounding tissues to the core of the matter.

'The Managers need £150,000 as £150,000 has seldom been needed before . . . So won't they have been in to get it? Into Branwell House? Into the lagging of the hot-water system or whatever? You've got a great deal of stuff here that will need a lot of proving, Kenworthy.'

Kenworthy looked at him with wide, innocent eyes.

'We shall have to persuade them to tell us about it themselves, shan't we?' he said. 'Damn it, with three of them at Grendon, and Stephens under lock and key, and Webbe under lock and key, and the money at Branwell House for us to walk in and get—if we can't trip somebody up over that lot, we ought to stop trying. It's a pity so much had to devolve on poor Webbe. Stephens clearly managed the Morley Mortain holiday; that was done with finesse. He left the Norfolk farmers to Webbe; and Webbe could manage them, even with the rag, tag and bobtail bunch he had as his guards. But the women defeated him: Stephens had threatened him with God knows what if any of them came to harm. The real job was done, you see, and he didn't see to taking unnecessary risks.'

They looked again at the potted biographies.

MAYBURY, John Watkins: Aged 50, married, two grown-up children, whereabouts unknown; domiciled north London. Two custodial offences, separated by 15 years: obtaining pecuniary advantage by deception; destroying a record made for accounting purposes.

'The pecuniary advantage,' Kenworthy said, 'was a firm's time-sheets. Maybury was a senior wages-clerk and was splitting differences with his mates over falsifications.

He went a long time before he tripped up again. The second time, he'd got rid of books that would have been of great interest to an Official Receiver, since they showed preferential settlement of debts when insolvency was inescapable.'

Maybury pulled a wry face when he was told that he was for interview downstairs with a London copper.

'Kenworthy again?'

Maybury did not care for Kenworthy, but up to now had been able to handle him.

'No. Forrester,' the screw said.

'Forrester? Christ! He's Sweeney, isn't he?'

And Forrester towered over Maybury, giving the impression of a man who had been bogged down in paperwork just a little too long for his mental health; a man happy to be back on the ground.

'We won't mess about, Maybury. Just describe how you and that dentist topped Franky.'

'Honestly, Mr Forrester, I had nothing to do with it.'

'*It*. What's *it* mean?'

'That dentist—he came up about choppers for me. I've never had false choppers in my life—'

'I know all about that. Who let him in? A screw?'

'Yes. Evans. Left the door open. Because Leigh and Evans had a brag school going—and when one of them's winning, that's all they want to know about. And—'

There can be a relief in confession, especially when a man has had a very long time to live with its content. In those circumstances, even partial confession can be a comfort. It can be lubricated when a frightened little man like Maybury is afraid that a giant like Forrester is about to set about him: which looked as if it were the case.

'And, Maybury—?'

'Well, sir, this dentist had a key, and he wanted me to come with him to see Franky. And I wouldn't.'

'Why wouldn't you?'

'I didn't want to get mixed up in it.'

'Are you sitting there trying to get me to believe that Bryce told you in advance what he was going to do?'

'I could see he was up to no good.'

'Maybury, Bryce was a prison official, as far as you were concerned. Do you normally think that prison dentists are up to no good?'

Forrester raised a large, red, hairy hand. It went to stroke his chin.

'You went with him, Maybury.'

'But I didn't do anything. It was Bryce who did it all.'

'You just held his arms, perhaps? Diverted his attention. All right, take your time, Maybury. It will be good for you to get it out of your system. There's a difference between destroying evidence of preferential debts and getting mixed up in this sort of thing.'

'If I hadn't been put into this bloody place, Mr Forrester—'

It was only incidentally that the fact came to light that the creditor who had done best out of Maybury's white-collar crime had been a man called Scales, to whom premiums were owing by the firm that could not continue to trade.

Hewitson arrived at Grendon Underwood with a much bigger back-up force than the task surely called for.

Waterlow, Scales and Ulliatt were again carting logs on a farm on the main Aylesbury-Bicester Road. It was their tea-break and the farmer's wife, a sympathetic soul, had made doughnuts at Scales's request. Waterlow ate his apart from the others. Hewitson cautioned the three while they were still eating.

'£150,000? Is that how much there was supposed to be?'

One never knew with Lil Tasker when the truth shaded

off into some devious policy or other.

'Oh, they didn't fool me,' she said. 'Couple came round saying they were from the Water Board, which I didn't believe for a minute—wanted to look at the plumbing. Went straight to the airing cupboard. There was only one reason why anyone should be interested in my airing cupboard. Of course, the lagging was all gone. Disappeared months ago. There's a laugh for you, Mr Kenworthy—the mice had had it. Eaten practically every shred of the packing.'

'And I suppose they'd eaten £150,000 as well?'

'Nibbled into it. You know—Franky and mice—it's as if he'd known all his life that they'd do him out of his last takings.'

There was a blade-edged silence in the flat in Branwell House. Everyone knew that some shock of revelation was about to come. Lil Tasker was not to be done out of her little moment of dramatic build-up. Saying very little in a corner, Jackie was wearing a colour-drained housecoat, and her head was weighed down under a turban of towel. She was obviously in a stage of transition, but it was not apparent from what to what.

'So what's happened to the mice's leavings?' Kenworthy asked.

'Where they belong. You might say, in a way, where they started out from. In a bank deposit. You wouldn't think they'd let a dead-beat old woman like me have a safe in a vault, would you? They'll let you have anything, if you pay for it. Anyway—I put the stuff away, Mr Kenworthy. Till the dust had cleared—'

'You mean now that you know the Manager won't be calling you to account for it,' Kenworthy said.

Jackie gave a little laugh: artificial—but there was at least a touch of hysteria about it.

'Open-ended to the finish, Mum. But you were an idiot. When those two men didn't find what they came for—'

'Oh, they were stupid,' Lil Tasker said. 'No imagination. They cut their losses and stuck to the story they were from the Water Board. I heard one say to the other, "Well, I never believed there was anything there. Laughing gas!" Things would have happened differently in the old days.'

There was a strong faction in the Bishop's Fold Institute who really did think that they ought to have a change and go to Scarborough next year. But Southport won the day again. The President did not believe in bad luck. It was discipline that counted.

Business returned to its idle norm in the boutique of Millicent Mayhew. Sometimes when she walks across the meadows at the end of the day, inured by now to the sulphurous dust blowing over and down from the brick-fields, her mind turns towards tanned Mediterranean men.

The Parish Council at Binney St Botolph waited until a newcomer's illicit trellis porch was blown down in a gale, then passed a resolution requiring him to remove it.